DATE DUE

F
Hol   Holland, Isabelle
        The Unfrightened dark

The
Unfrightened
Dark

The Unfrightened Dark

A NOVEL BY

Isabelle Holland

LITTLE, BROWN AND COMPANY

Boston Toronto London

Library of Congress Cataloging-in-Publication Data
Holland, Isabelle.
    The unfrightened dark: a novel/by Isabelle Holland. — 1st ed.
        p.   cm.
    Summary: When her beloved guide dog is kidnapped, Jocelyn,
orphaned and blind since the age of twelve, determines to solve the
mystery surrounding his disappearance.
    ISBN 0-316-37173-4
    [1. Blind — Fiction.   2. Physically handicapped — Fiction.
3. Mystery and detective stories.]   I. Title.
PZ7.H7083Un   1990   89-31570
[Fic] — dc19   CIP
                                                          AC

10 9 8 7 6 5 4 3 2 1

HC

Published simultaneously in Canada
by Little, Brown & Company (Canada) Limited

PRINTED IN THE UNITED STATES OF AMERICA

The Unfrightened Dark

There had been no sound of traffic and then, frighteningly, there was the wild screech of tires. I felt Brace's body move across my legs to prevent me from going forward. Almost at the same moment I instinctively leaned over, putting my arms in front of Brace to protect him. The speeding car passed so near I could feel the wind against my face and neck.

"He did that on purpose," I whispered to Brace when I could talk. I felt Brace's warm body against mine tremble. If I could have laid my hands on the driver, I think I would have killed him. I love Brace more than anything in the world. He's my companion and my best friend. He is also a golden retriever and my guide dog. I've been blind since I was twelve, but I got him only a year ago, when I turned sixteen, the youngest age the leading guide dog training people will allow anyone to have one of their dogs. Our friendship may only be a year old, but I can't imagine my life without Brace.

"Good dog," I said, and stroked him. "Good dog!"

"What an unspeakable person!" a woman's voice said next to me. "And what a wonderful dog!"

I love to hear Brace praised. "Yes, he's wonderful," I said. "Who was driving the car?"

"Nobody I've ever seen in Brinton! I can't believe it! Just starting up like that!"

"You mean from standing?"

"Yes. He was parked there beside the movie house and then boom — for no reason!"

"Well, he's gone now." I smiled a little. "Good-bye." Then I said to Brace, "Forward." I'd been automatically listening for the cessation of traffic so Brace and I could cross. I was still a little scared for both Brace and me, but what had happened was rare and I couldn't let it stop us from walking on the sidewalks and crossing the streets. After all, I had to go to school every day, and was lucky that Brace and I lived with Aunt Marion in the middle of Brinton and were in walking distance of almost everything. Also, of course, I knew Brace would refuse to go if there was any danger in front of me — as he'd just shown — or something like an open manhole or an overhang that I'd hit my head on.

So I forgot about the car until much later, when I had reason to remember it.

When you're blind, you learn that people often either forget you're blind and ask indignantly, "Can't you read?" and then go into paroxysms of remorse for being so insensitive, or they want to do everything for you, to protect you from every wind that blows. Of the two, the second is the harder to put up with.

Somebody who doesn't do either is Pip Mowbray, who is in my class at St. Stephen's School. That is, he's in my class when he's not absent for reasons nobody seems to know, or is cutting class for reasons like going to the movies. It's not that he's not bright. He's very bright and as a consequence either gets A's or F's — nothing in between.

Once when our classroom teacher pointed this out in front

of a bunch of us, Pip said, "But, Mr. Langton, everybody knows that the middle is boring."

"It's also boring not to be able to get into a college that you want to go to," Mr. Langton said.

"I'm beginning to think that going to college is boring," Pip said. I heard his sneakered feet scrape against the floor as he said that, so I supposed he was slouching lower at his desk. It's amazing how many things you can pick up by hearing.

"Hiya," Pip said now as Brace and I drew nearer the school. "How's tricks?"

"Fine. How're yours?"

There was a short silence. I knew from where his voice was placed that he had fallen in beside me.

"Not so good?" I asked again.

"Not great. My enchanting parent has fallen off the wagon again, I think I'm going to flunk English, and Dad is threatening to sell Boucher if I don't at least graduate. He's long given up on my grades being anywhere except in the lowest tenth, but, as I point out, one obsessive cum laude in the family is enough. No point in being greedy."

Of all of these I was pretty sure he was most upset by the threat to Boucher, who was his horse. Boucher is the only creature for whom Pip will actually admit affection.

"Personally," he went on, "I think it's because Boucher bit one of Dad's more disgusting business associates that he brought home last weekend."

"What was the business associate doing to Boucher?" I asked.

"Getting overfriendly, like trying to ride him. Boucher is particular about who rides him."

I had once been up on Boucher myself when Pip had led me over to him and helped me mount. He'd put Boucher on a lead rein and hung onto it while he was mounting another horse and we'd gone for a fairly sedate ride. I'd longed to dig my feet into Boucher's side and have him gallop, but I knew I didn't dare. Horses are not trained in what the guide dog people call "intelligent disobedience," which meant that I could easily have been knocked out of the saddle by a tree branch while Boucher would have galloped happily under it. Brace, now, wouldn't let that happen to me even if I gave the signal for "Forward."

"Would your father really sell Boucher?" I asked now.

There was a pause. "Probably not. He's just trying any and all arguments to get me to buckle down, Winsocki, buckle down."

"Why don't you?" I asked, knowing it would irritate him.

"Because I don't feel like it," he said abruptly.

"Hi, Pip, hi, Jocelyn!" That was Barbara Weldon. At the beginning of the year, when Barbara first arrived, I asked my friend Meg Reynolds what she looked like.

"Sort of like nothing waiting for nothing to happen," Meg had said, and then because she's kind, "That's an awful thing to say about anybody. She's plain, not very attractive . . ." She hesitated again. "That's even worse to say. I guess, what it is, she looks as though she'd be the first to agree with anybody who said that. It's like she knew it, but also knew there wasn't anything she could do about it."

Maybe because of this, Barbara's voice, until recently, had been so flat and depressed sounding I always wanted to say something idiotic like "It's going to be all right," or "Whatever it is you'll survive," or words to that effect.

Lately, though, she had sounded different. "Like maybe she has a boyfriend," Meg said. And her "Hi, Pip, hi, Jocelyn!" now sounded almost excited.

I'd tried once or twice to get to know Barbara, but she never seemed to want me to get close. Since I wasn't blind till I was twelve, I remembered what people looked like, which made me sort of different from some of the students at the institute I went to right after the accident to learn how to walk with a cane and generally cope. Those who were born blind knew, theoretically, that people had differences in their faces, but couldn't really flesh out the idea — if you'll excuse the pun — while I knew because I had seen them. Now, when I got to know people really well, I'd ask them to let me touch their faces and I'd learned how to translate the feel of the face into a mental picture of what it looked like. But I never got to know Barbara that well. Nobody did, I guess. Not until it was too late.

"Hi, Barbara," I said, and went into the school.

During class Brace sits under my desk. Only once did this cause any comments. A substitute teacher suddenly raised her voice and said acidly, "I didn't know students were now allowed to bring pets to class."

At first it made me furious, but then I thought it was so awful and so dumb it was funny. Before I had a chance to say anything the entire class chanted, almost like a chorus, "Jocelyn's blind. That's her guide dog."

"Oh. I see. Well, make sure he doesn't interfere with your work, er, Jocelyn."

"Without him I wouldn't have any," I replied, irritated, because she was obviously too stupid to admit what a goof she'd made.

"What a jerk!" Meg said afterward. "They must have really reached into the attic for her."

Meg is my best friend. Her father is the local vet and a great fan of Brace's.

"Hi, Joss. Hi, Brace," she said this morning as Pip and I walked into the classroom.

"Hello, Meg," Pip said.

"Hello."

It's funny about voices. They do for me what smiles and

facial expressions do for other people — that is, they give me an idea of what people are thinking or feeling. Meg's "hello" to Pip was about three degrees colder than her greeting to me. That much didn't surprise me. I'd learned from Meg that most of the girls in the school considered Pip desperately attractive.

"Do you?" I once asked Meg.

"Yes," she said abruptly, and then sighed. "You know, Joss, this is probably a gross thing to say, but sometimes I think you're kind of — well — lucky. I mean," she went on hastily, "every girl here is flat on her face in love with Pip. But you can't see him, so he doesn't have that effect on you, does he?"

"No," I said. "What's it like — to be in love? I mean, people have described it in books, but . . ."

"It's like being in heaven and wanting to die at the same time. Much good it does me."

"Is he in love with anyone?" I asked.

"There's a rumor that he's getting it on with a girl from Meridan who works at the McDonald's or the malt shop down in the mall. I don't know how many that makes he's been cozy with. There seems to be a new one every few weeks. It's enough to make a nice, faithful type like me commit suicide out of sheer despair! Oh, well, I wish the school would hurry up and throw him out, I could then get on with my work studying for the SATs. He likes you, doesn't he?"

"We're friends," I said. And we were. He was always nice to me.

Meg sighed. "I'd settle for that — I think!"

Ever since then Meg has put a touch of ice in her voice when she spoke to him. I could hear it there this morning.

But there was another note in Meg's voice that bothered me. "Is something wrong?"

"I couldn't find Boomer this morning." Boomer was her

cat, a large, squishy, mostly black neutered male with big ears and long whiskers.

"Couldn't he have just found something fascinating and been delayed getting home?"

"That's what Dad kept saying. But, Joss, he's never been out all night before. He always sleeps on my bed. And I haven't seen him since right after dinner."

A strange fear went through me. I couldn't imagine what I'd do if Brace wandered off after dinner, after I'd taken off his harness, and never came back. But I knew he wouldn't do that. Something would have to prevent him from returning to me. "Why don't you call now and see if he's back?"

"I just did, but Mom's at work, so nobody's home and you know what a vet's phone is like — busy, busy, busy." Then she took a breath and said, "I keep trying to think positive, that Dad is right and Boomer's somewhere checking out the mouse situation."

An hour later Brace and I headed towards the cafeteria for lunch.

The cafeteria was, as always, a bit of a challenge. Brace would lead me between the tables to the beginning of the line, where I'd put a tray on the railing in front of the food. Whoever was behind serving would tell me what was offered that day, although I nearly always took a sandwich. At the end, where I paid, one of the helpers would take the tray and usually sit me down beside one of the people in my class, or some kid would come up and say "Sit with us, Jocelyn," take my tray and lead me over.

This time it was Pip. "Allow me," he said, taking the tray from my hands. "Come and join the elite!"

"Shall we, Brace?" I said.

"Actually, it's really Brace we want, but we knew we'd have to take you, too. This way." He led me over to his table. "Sit!" he said.

9

I could feel the back of the chair put gently behind my knees. I sat down. "Come on, Brace, sit," I said, and pushed him under my chair, where his paws were safe from being trod on.

"Hi," Meg's voice said from across the table. "I'm sitting opposite you. I thought Barbara was supposed to eat with us, but she hasn't shown. I guess she doesn't mind missing lunch." She sighed. "She sure isn't the enthusiastic eater I am."

"In a perfect world," Pip said, "all the people who want to lose weight would hate eating and all those who want to put it on would love it. But then nobody asked me when the whole thing was being thought up."

"A terrible oversight," I said solemnly. "And I could have thought up an improvement or two," I added, meaning to be funny. But it didn't quite come out that way.

"I bet," Meg said.

Pip's hand ruffled my hair.

I was suddenly intensely aware of how Meg felt about Pip — as though I were sitting across the table in her skin. I also knew, as though I were in Pip's mind, that he'd never ruffle Meg's hair, because with her it would mean something different. I sat frozen with a tumble of feelings, my hand squeezed around my sandwich.

Then three things happened, one right after the other.

Pip said in an odd voice, "Why are you trying to murder your sandwich?"

And the voice of a girl at the next table said into a small island of silence, "He's just nice to her because she's blind."

And one of the teachers suddenly materialized at my elbow. "Does anyone here know where Barbara Weldon is? She was supposed to be in the head's office an hour ago."

Barbara hadn't been located by the time I left school that afternoon. Her mother, hysterical and angry, was in the front hall shortly after lunch. I knew because I asked Meg, with whom I was going back to class, what the noise was.

"Somebody's yelling and sobbing in there," I said, as we passed the swing doors into the front part of the school.

"Mrs. Weldon," Meg said. "At least, that's the scuttlebutt. I look at Madame Weldon and I understand right away why Barbara's such a mouse."

"What's Mrs. Weldon like?" I asked.

"Rigid, knows what's best for everybody in every way, and from what I could gather, grades all Barbara's friends from minimally acceptable to forbidden."

"Horribly religious, I suppose," I said, thinking of my aunt, Marion Hunter, an Episcopal priest, who was sometimes dictatorial in her own way.

"The funny thing is, no," Meg said. We were walking across the campus back to class. Brace was on his lead, not wearing his harness, so he was acting more like a dog-dog and less like a guide dog. He was sniffing here and there, looking up, woofing when he saw something that interested him, like a cat or a ball or a squirrel, and poking around

11

fascinating items like trees. Meg described all of this as she acted as my guide, with my hand on her arm. She went on, "I think Mrs. Weldon is what my father calls a profound, dedicated atheist. She doesn't approve of religion or church, but has iron views about everything — like what kind of people make a good society, et cetera, et cetera, and wants Barbara to associate only with those."

"Is that why Barbara always sounds so downtrodden?"

"I think so."

"What about Mr. Weldon?"

"I think he's too cowed to do anything. Or maybe he agrees with his wife."

When we finished class Pip dropped by my locker when I was putting my books away and said, "Want a ride home?"

"No, thanks, Pip. It's only a mile and Brace and I need the exercise."

"Okay, but if it rains you'll be sorry."

"It's not going to rain."

"Ah so, Ms. Weatherwoman? How do you know?"

I couldn't really have given him a good reason. It was a combination of smelling the air and feeling it, that is, feeling how heavy it was on my face. When I tried to explain this once to Aunt Marion she replied rather curtly that it sounded to her like voodoo, so I had kept my weather comments mostly to myself.

"It must be wonderful to have the school's most attractive guy always at your service," a female voice I didn't recognize said.

"Oh, it is," I agreed. "Who are you?"

"Nobody important."

"But somebody who likes to hide behind the fact that I can't see your face."

"The fuss people make of you and your pet! I shouldn't think you'd feel left out."

"But you do," I said. "Or you wouldn't be talking this way. And Brace isn't a pet. He's a working dog."

"Poor thing! Never off the harness!"

"What do you mean? Of course he gets off the harness! Who *are* you?"

Pause. Then: "My name's Sandy Martin."

I hadn't heard the name before, though that didn't mean anything. "Are you new?"

"No, I just don't move with your crowd. Too rich for my blood. Good-bye."

It was a weird encounter, and upsetting. Most people fell over themselves to let me know who they were and anything else that would be helpful. I decided to ask Meg what she knew about Sandy Martin as soon as she got home and I could call her. Meg always stayed today for an extra lab class but I had to get home for my piano lesson.

There's piano music in braille that I study. I also listen to tapes, and, if I can trick him into it, I get my teacher, Jeremy Stoddard, to play through the pieces I am learning. If he does it often enough, I can learn by rote, but he doesn't like to do that. He wants me to be able to read music properly. He also plays the organ at church and teaches me that, too. Sometimes, when he knows he's going to be away, he asks me to play for a service.

He was there, waiting for me, when Brace and I reached the house. I could hear him playing as we came up the front drive. Brace and I were as quiet as we could be, but the moment he heard us come into the room he stopped.

"Hello," he said, and then when I had taken off Brace's harness: "Hi, Brace! Can I pat him?"

"Yes. He's being all dog now, so you can pat him."

"Good boy," Jeremy said. And then: "How's the Schumann?"

13

"All right. It's a bit slow going. I wish you'd play it for me."

"That's the lazy way. You'll never learn how to read if you have me play things for you first."

The moment Jeremy said that I realized he sounded like himself for the first time since I walked in. Until then there'd been a constraint, what I call a sort of down sound, in his voice. If he were somebody from school I'd have said, "What's the matter?" But though I like Jeremy a lot, he's Aunt Marion's age, and there's a reserve about him that made me hesitate.

Still, at the end of the lesson I heard myself say, "Are you okay, Jeremy?"

There was a tiny pause, then he said, "Fine, why?"

"I just thought . . . it doesn't matter."

Aunt Marion walked in at that moment. "Hello, Jocelyn, hello, Jeremy. Could I speak to you about the hymns on Sunday before you go, Jeremy?"

"Of course."

"Hello, Brace," Aunt Marion said, and then, to me, "Shouldn't he be outside? I mean, he's not wearing his harness?"

I opened my mouth to answer when she added, "However, you know best. Now, Jeremy, shall we go back to my study?"

If it were not for Aunt Marion, my father's half sister, I'd be in some kind of institution by now. Right after the accident that killed my parents and blinded me she showed up at the hospital and said that of course I was going to live with her. Although she has never said — or even implied — that having me has been an expense she can barely afford, I know it's true and that she has a hard time squeezing out household money. I also know I couldn't even think of going to St. Stephen's School if I weren't there on a special scholarship that was probably arranged by Aunt Marion. She spends a lot of her time helping out with the homeless, who seem to have increased in number here as they have elsewhere, and she's known for her charitable works to the needy of the parish and the community. Yet —

It's the "yet" that's like a wall between us, keeping us from really being friends. But if I tried to describe what the "yet" is, about the only thing I could say is she doesn't like Brace. As a matter of fact, she doesn't much like animals of any kind. When people ooh and ah over how wonderful Brace is and what an aid he is and how wonderful guide dogs are and so on and on, she curtly agrees. "Truly remarkable," she says, and changes the subject.

Once I said to her, "You don't like Brace."

"What nonsense," she said. "Of course I do. When I think of how much he helps you —"

"Yes, but you don't like him." I underlined the word in my voice.

"As you know, I'm allergic," she said. And she is. That is, when she's around us I've heard her sniff and blow her nose. So I try to keep Brace on the other side of the room, or I would if he didn't stay away from her on his own. It's strange, because when Brace isn't working, he's the world's friend, to the point where I sometimes worry about it — when I am thinking up things to worry about. Yet he's only polite to Aunt Marion, polite but unenthusiastic.

Once when I was trying to get to the bottom of how Aunt Marion feels about Brace I said, "Maybe it's because he's a golden retriever. Maybe you don't like golden retrievers —"

"I have told you I don't dislike Brace, and I don't want to hear any more about it. If there's anything I'm doing wrong, please tell me, but if I'm not, don't bring up the subject again."

"All right," I said, swallowing resentment. "I'm sorry."

"It's all right."

And that night, even though she loathes cooking, she went to the kitchen and baked a chocolate cake for me. I wished she hadn't. I adore chocolate, but I hate feeling that she's putting herself out to make amends like that.

Usually we get on pretty well. I help once a week in the parish hall kitchen on a day when the homeless are fed. When I first volunteered Aunt Marion pooh-poohed the idea. "You might hurt yourself, you know."

"I can learn to find my way around there. After all, I do in school."

"Yes, but there are pots of hot water in the kitchen and hot stews and soups and things like that."

"I don't have to be around them, and anyway I can't go through life not handling hot pots of one kind or another."

"I don't think you should do it here."

And that would have been the end of it, if I hadn't talked to Mrs. Brent, who's on the feeding committee. I carefully didn't tell her what Aunt Marion had said. I just said I'd like to help out. So Aunt Marion walked in one day, and there I was helping to dole out the food, with Brace sitting behind me.

"You might give out the wrong food," Aunt Marion said.

"If she does, they'll tell her fast enough," Mrs. Brent said.

And Brace, when he was off the harness, was a great hit. I had to beg some of the people not to feed him.

I asked Mrs. Brent if Aunt Marion had objected.

"Not objected, exactly," Mrs. Brent said. "Just filled with reservations and rather ominous warnings."

"I can't understand it. I've lived with her now for five years. She knows I can do an awful lot, that I'm not made of fragile glass and won't shatter into a thousand pieces."

"She probably does, but I think she sometimes has a hard time with the more mundane aspects of life."

"What do you mean?"

"I guess I mean I think of her as a frustrated activist. She's very good with causes — you know, like the homeless, other social issues. She cares a lot about them. But her mental focus is so much on them, she may be a little inclined to overlook an individual who isn't part of a cause, standing next to her. Like you. Great idealists are often like that. I think if she had a choice she'd be at a barricade somewhere."

I tried to imagine Aunt Marion at a barricade. I knew, because I remembered her from before the accident, that she was of medium height, sort of stocky with short dark hair and rather fiery dark eyes. Thinking about it, I decided Mrs. Brent was right. Aunt Marion would be happy on a barricade.

"All right. So she really wants to be a revolutionary. But what's that got to do with not liking Brace?"

"I don't think she dislikes him. He's just not part of what she's looking at now."

I love walking, especially in the afternoon and especially with Brace pulling me at a fast clip. As long as he's leading I know I'm not going to bump into anything or fall over or into anything.

Back of the house is open country leading down to the river that runs into the harbor and then up some low hills. I like to go walking there with Brace.

"Come along, Brace," I said after Jeremy had left with Aunt Marion, "let's go wogging" — which is my term for walking so fast that sometimes, depending on the surface, I break into a minor jog. I put on my running shoes and strapped Brace into his harness. Then I headed for the back door. "Forward," I said.

It was a beautiful day in October. I could feel the sun on my face and the gentle but pleasant breeze. There's much talk about the silence of the open country. Actually, it's teeming with small noises: the twittering of the birds, the sounds of various insects, the rustle of leaves as the wind blows through them and the unmistakable lapping of water. The air smelled fresh, not wet, so I was fairly sure it wouldn't rain. (Besides, I had listened to the forecast on my little transistor radio before I left.) I would have about two hours before it was dark. Although light and dark were the same to me, they weren't to the world of sighted people. After dark, Aunt Marion started worrying more then ever. Once when I pointed out that I couldn't tell the difference, she replied that other people were known to do things in the dark that they wouldn't do in daylight.

We zigzagged down towards the water, taking a path that would eventually lead into a small bridge across the river. I followed Brace and talked to him about this and that as we went along. He didn't go straight, he led me slightly left and right, taking me around various small holes or rocks or whatever kept the path from being totally smooth.

"Let's go to the bridge," I said, knowing Brace would understand because he'd been there. "But after that let's come back and go along the river road to the beginning of the piers." I added, because she'd been on my mind, "I wonder if Mrs. Weldon has calmed down yet."

I don't know what happened then. There was no noise I could possibly define as such. But I suddenly became certain that someone was standing not far off. In a room there are lots of explanations why a blind person can detect the presence of someone there — sound bouncing off a surface

18

nearer than usual, the slight alteration in the echoing. Why I was sure now there was somebody near me outside, I don't know. Then Brace growled. I had never heard him do that before.

"Who is it? Who's there?" I called sharply.

There were sounds of footsteps running down and away from me.

I am lucky in that I am seldom frightened. But as I felt the sudden thump of my heart, I knew fear.

I was still a little shaken when Brace and I went to lunch the next day in the cafeteria, and was pleasantly surprised when Pip greeted me at the door, where he was waiting for me. After guiding me around the food table he carried my tray to a table. I was pretty sure we were at the table alone, but I said, "Just us?"

"Just us," he said. "Hope you don't mind."

"Not a bit, but where's Meg?"

"Dunno, haven't seen her. Maybe she's got a class."

"I guess so." But I was surprised. I knew Meg's schedule almost as well as I knew mine, and she didn't usually have a class at this time. Then suddenly I remembered Barbara. "What's the news about Barbara? Has she shown up?"

"Not as far as I know. As you've no doubt heard, because everyone else has, too, her mother was here weeping and wailing in the front hall, saying she was now convinced Barbara hadn't been home the night before."

"If she's such a perfect and strict mother, how come she didn't know?"

"A good question. Something about Mrs. Weldon having been out to some kind of good works meeting and assuming when she got home that Barbara was in bed. In fact, I seem to remember somebody who overheard said she'd checked

Barbara's bedroom and seen that she was, indeed, in bed. But the next morning, when Barbara didn't show, she went in and saw that it was just clothes bunched up to look like she was in bed."

"Wow! That really sounds like she took off! Well, from what Meg told me, who can blame her?"

"Yeah, I guess so. Better to have a parent like mine who's drunk half the time."

"You sound bitter."

"I can't think why."

I thought for a moment. "Alcoholism is supposed to be a disease."

"So? You mean somebody forced open her mouth and poured the stuff down against her will?"

The picture was so wild I giggled.

"You see now what I mean!"

I did, but I still thought that I'd rather have a Mrs. Mowbray, even drunk, than the kind of mother who laid out your entire life. This made me think about my own mother, who had been the opposite. She expected me to behave, but she always said she wanted me to be free.

I was twelve the night that she and Daddy and I were driving back from dinner at a country inn. She'd just made one of her dry, funny comments about a pompous-sounding man at the next table who had objected to almost everything the waiter had brought and had reduced the poor waiter to silent rage.

Daddy turned and looked at her. He was laughing, too, but he said, "Where's your charity?"

"At the moment, it's about on a par with that dreadful man's humility!"

Daddy gave a shout of laughter. That was the last I ever saw of either of them, their faces turned to each other, smiling. From all accounts our car was hit by an oncoming trailer truck that had veered out of its lane. I woke up about a week later in the local hospital, my eyes and head bandaged. As slowly as they could, the doctors and nurses let me know that my parents had been killed and that I would never see again.

For years it was so painful to think of either of them, but especially Mother, that I spent a good deal of time and effort trying not to.

"How do I love you? Let me count the ways."

Elizabeth Barrett Browning was talking about her husband when she wrote that. But I always think about Mother when I hear it, because this was one of the things she used to read to me. She adored poetry and Daddy always teased her about being vain about her voice. . . .

"Hey! HEY!" I felt Pip's hand on my arm. "What did I say?"

"What do you mean?" I said, and was embarrassed to feel tears on my cheek.

"What did I say to make you cry? The entire cafeteria is looking at me like I'm Attila the Hun!"

"You didn't say anything. I'm sorry, really!" And I reached out my own hand and grasped his arm. "I was thinking about Mother. That happens sometimes. I guess — I feel like a fool!"

"That's better than feeling like your local friendly torturer."

I giggled and then felt a piece of material pushed into my hand.

"It's clean," Pip said. "For once."

For a moment I thought he'd also put his hand on my knee, then realized it was Brace's head. He does that when I'm upset, and he always knows when that is, because he always knows exactly how I feel. I rubbed his head.

"Thanks," I said to Pip, mopping up. I felt stupid and embarrassed.

That afternoon I decided to walk home via the shopping mall. I needed to go to the cassette store to get some blank tapes. When I'm in class I can take notes in one of two ways, with something called a slate and stylus, where I can write in braille by punching the metal slate with a thin stylus, or by taping what the teacher is saying on a small tape recorder. Of the two I preferred tapes, and I'd just about run out.

As Brace and I walked towards the mall I tried to figure out why I was thinking about Mother in such an intense way at lunch. It had been a long time since I'd had a reaction like that. I went over everything that had happened since I entered the cafeteria, but nothing came to mind. Except for Meg's not being there, nothing could have been more ordinary.

That reminded me that I hadn't seen Meg during the afternoon, either. It's true we didn't have class together, but it was unusual for us not to get together for a minute or two at some point in the afternoon, in the halls or by the lockers. I wasn't aware of anything being wrong — and then I remembered Boomer, her cat, who hadn't come home.

"We're going to have to call about Boomer, Brace," I said.

At that moment we reached the main street and Brace sat down at the curb, waiting until it was safe to take me across.

It was when I was in the store, waiting for the clerk to wrap up the tapes, that a young male voice said beside me, "That's a beautiful dog you have there."

"Thank you," I said. "But please don't pat him. He's working."

"It's such a shame," the voice went on, "that he has to be imprisoned in your blindness."

I was stunned, angry and bewildered, all at once. "I don't imprison him. When he's not working, he stays by me of his own accord. Anyway, retrievers are working dogs." As I said the words I suddenly remembered I had said them before to someone — quite recently, but I couldn't remember to whom.

"Only because human beings have made them work," the young man said now. "They should be free, the way we all want to be free."

"Hey," the clerk said, coming back. "What the hell are you saying? Who are you, anyway?"

"Just an animal lover. Au revoir, Brace, I'll be seeing you." And I heard steps going out.

Whether it was his voice or his words I didn't know, but it was as though a cold wind went through me. "Brace," I whispered, "Brace," and put my hand on his head. Standing in the store, I had been holding his lead, not his harness, so he felt free to lick my hand. Then I knelt down and put my arm around him and he licked my cheek.

"I'm sorry, Jocelyn," the clerk said. "I didn't know that jerk was going to to threaten you."

"He didn't threaten me. He threatened Brace. And how did he know his name? Who is he? I've never heard his voice before."

"I dunno. I mean, I don't know who he is. I've seen him around a couple of times."

"Does anybody you know know him?"

"No. If I find out, I'll let you know. But I'd just write him off as a nut. Honest!"

But I didn't think I could write him off.

* * *

Sometime in the middle of that night I woke up with my heart pounding. "Brace," I whispered, and dropped my hand over the side of the bed to where he always slept in his own bed beside mine. Immediately I felt his tongue licking my hand. Then there was a cushiony growl from my own bed, and Cyrus, my big Maine coon cat, came up beside me and climbed on top of me and lay down. "Thanks a lot," I said, but stroked and rubbed his head.

Cyrus had been picked off the side of the road by some well-wisher who thought he had been run over and killed. He had been run over, but he wasn't dead, so his rescuer took him to the veterinary clinic, left some money to cover expenses and disappeared. Meg's father put him up for adoption. One day, when I was there with Brace, he walked out of the hospital part into the waiting room, rubbed against my legs, meowed and jumped on my lap. I decided to adopt him, and because he was long-haired and fuzzy I called him Cyrus, after Cyrus, King of the Persians.

"But he's not a Persian," Dr. Reynolds objected, when he was giving him his shots. "He's almost certainly a Maine coon."

"But he's got long hair and he's still a king," I said.

"I thought I told you I was allergic," Aunt Marion said that evening when I brought him home. She sounded bewildered rather than angry.

I immediately felt guilty because I had forgotten all about it.

"I'll keep him in my room," I said hastily and took him up there at once.

He and Brace took a while to become friends. But one night, when I put my hand down to feel Brace beside me, I also felt a large, plump, long-haired object curled up next to him. Since then Cyrus spends half his nights in bed with me, and the other half in bed with Brace.

I lay there for a while, one hand on Brace, the other on Cyrus. My heartbeat had gone back to normal, and I was trying to remember whatever I had dreamed that had sent it galloping. Nothing came to mind, but I remembered suddenly when I had told someone that Brace was a working dog. It was by my locker when I was speaking to the girl who said she was Sandy Martin.

I had been so upset by the encounter in the cassette store that I had forgotten to call Meg about Boomer. So as soon as I heard her voice in class the next day I said, "Has Boomer come back?"

"No," she said. "And I'm sick about it. I've gone out looking for him everywhere and the guys in the ambulance have kept an eye out for him. But nothing — not even, well, his body if he was hurt or killed. And it's not like him! He's not an adventurous cat. He's never gone wandering off." She sounded on the point of tears.

"What does your dad say?"

"He's said he's terribly sorry and he hopes he gets back soon, but I could tell by the way he said it he didn't think he would. Dad hasn't said so, but I think he thinks Boomer was stolen."

"But why? I mean — I know he's a wonderful cat — almost as great as Cyrus. But he's not a pedigree or anything."

"People steal them and sell them to labs."

"Yes," I said, feeling sick. I knew it was true. I just prayed and prayed that it hadn't happened to Boomer, and then sent up another prayer about Cyrus. Cyrus went out all the time. For a moment I toyed with the idea of keeping him inside for a while. But I knew I couldn't do it. Feeling the way I do about being free . . . and then I remembered that man in the video store.

"Meg," I said. "A weird thing happened yesterday when I was in the cassette store." And I told her about the man.

"What a creep," she said. "Sometimes I think the human race is made up largely of nuts and weirdos."

"I told Aunt Marion about the man at dinner last night. She said she understood how he could think people exploit animals. But Meg, I don't exploit Brace. He has a wonderful life. If he were roaming free like that dingbat said, he'd be starving, like all those wretched strays in places like the South Bronx, where dogs that have been abandoned hunt in packs and so on. I don't know why Aunt Marion said that. But it was dumb of me to tell her. She's not into animals. I once told her I didn't think she liked Brace. She denied it, but she changed the subject. And I still think she doesn't like him."

"How could she not like him? I mean, that's crazy. You don't have to be an animal nut to realize what a terrific dog he is and how important he is to you."

"Mrs. Brent — one of the women in the church who's active in the feeding program — once said she thought Aunt Marion was cause-minded."

"What did she mean?"

"You know, an activist. She said she'd probably be happiest on a barricade."

"What's that got to do with Brace?"

"I don't know. But it's the only reason I can think of that she'd defend that man in the cassette shop." There was a short pause. I was upset all over again, not only about Boomer, but about the man in the store and Brace, and, I realized now, about Aunt Marion. "She's been so good to me, Meg, I mean, without her I'd be in some institute for the blind or a foster home or something, because she's the only relative my parents had. But —"

"But she's a cold fish."

"Is it just me, or do you feel it, too?"

Meg said slowly, "It depends, I guess, on what you talk to her about. Daddy once told her that he almost named the clinic Saint Francis's Clinic, because even though he's not Catholic or anything, he always loved Saint Francis for what he felt about animals. You know what your aunt said? She said it was a pity his good works for people weren't equally well known."

"I bet she did. But, Meg, don't tell anybody what I said. Because she has done so much for me."

At that moment the teacher walked in and we had to stop talking.

"Where's Pip?" I said at lunch. "It's hot dogs today and you know how he loves them."

"Haven't seen him," Meg said briefly. "He wasn't in any of his usual classes. Maybe the girl in the hamburger joint is keeping him out too late."

We were still eating when a girl's voice said, "Can I sit here?" and I recognized the voice of the girl, Sandy Martin, who had spoken to me. I stiffened, then made sure that Brace was safely tucked beneath my chair.

"Sorry I was rude the other day," Sandy said.

"It's okay," I replied, not thinking it was.

"What'd you say?" Meg asked.

"I made a crack about Jocelyn's being lucky to have the most attractive guy in the school running around waiting on her."

"Yeah, well, they're friends, aren't you, Jocelyn?"

"Yes. Nothing romantic."

"You mean you're his good work?"

I sucked in my breath.

"That's gross!" Meg said.

"What did I ever do to you?" I asked. "That's the second time you've said something bitchy to me and I don't think I ever even met you before."

"Oh, you've met me. You just wouldn't know it."

"Yes, I would. I remember voices."

"We haven't spoken. But sometimes at the shake counter in the mall — when you're usually with Pip, of course — I've made up some of your sodas. Unlike some people, I have to work for a living."

"You must have made up a lot of people's," Meg said. "Why pick on Jocelyn?"

"Excuse me. I guess I sat at the wrong table. Only the in crowd sit here." And I heard her scrape her chair back, plonk something on her tray and start to move away. Brace gave a faint whimper.

"Watch out for my dog," I snapped.

"The whole town watches out for your dog. You're Ms. Famous!" And with that she marched away.

"I don't understand," I said. "What has she got against me?"

"Maybe she's in love with Pip. Maybe she's one of the many Pip loved and ran away from. I know he's your buddy, but he's known for that."

Brace and I were walking home on the road skirting the mall when I heard the sound of brakes alongside and to the front. I started to stop, but Brace went right on, which made me realize that there was no threat to us. "Good boy!" I said. "Good boy," and leaned down and patted him.

"That's a great dog you have out there," a male voice said. "What'll you take for him?" With a sense of shock I

30

realized it was the same voice I'd heard in the cassette shop.

"Who are you?" I asked angrily. "Brace is my guide dog."

I heard the sound of people laughing, then there was a screech and the car took off.

I stood there, shaking and frightened.

"Are you all right?" another voice said near me.

"Did you see that? Those people in the car?"

"I saw a car drive off, but I'm afraid I didn't see anything else. Did they do something?"

"They —" But when I thought of repeating what they said, I realized that to somebody who wasn't blind, who didn't understand how I'd feel, to say "they admired my dog, said what a great dog he is" wouldn't sound like justification for my rage and fear.

"It doesn't matter," I said. "Thanks, anyway. Let's go, Brace."

It was about ten minutes later. I had passed the mall area and was on the lane leading to my house when I heard a car stop again. I could feel my heart beginning to pound. Then Pip's voice said, "It's usually useless to offer you a lift. Still, would you like a lift?"

"Yes," I said. "I would."

"I'll come get you."

"You don't have to. You're by the sidewalk, aren't you?"

"Yes. All right. It's only a couple of feet."

I heard him open the car door.

"Let's go, Brace. Into the car."

I put Brace in the back and then got in front.

Pip started up the car. "To what do I owe this honor? You're usually relentless about your exercise."

"Pip, weird things have been happening." I told him about the man in the cassette shop and in the car just now. "It makes me so afraid for Brace. I feel like, well, like I'm putting him in some kind of danger, just by using him. But he's such a part of my life that I don't know what to do to protect him."

"Weird is right. Well, I can talk to the clerk in the store. Who was it? Glen? Joe?"

"I'm not sure. Maybe the one I've heard people call Joe. At least, I think it might have been. But I could be wrong."

"I can find out. What about this yahoo? What kind of voice did he have? How old did he sound? Like a grown man or a kid?"

I thought for a moment. "Maybe late teens or early twenties."

Pip's questions showed me again — if I needed showing — what a good friend he'd been to me. Most people mean well. But Pip, and maybe Meg, were the only ones who were around me enough and had listened to me enough to know the kind of things to ask. "You're a good friend, Pip," I said. And put my hand on his arm.

He grasped it in his own hand. Then he said, "Don't distract the driver! . . . Well," he said after a minute, "anything interesting about the creep's voice or how he spoke?"

I tried to think back. "Who are the people who say 'aboot the hoose'? Not as exaggerated as that, but sort of."

"Canadians and Tidewater Virginians. Did he have a southern accent apart from that?"

"He actually said so few words, I can't really be sure. But maybe."

"Okay. Your friendly sleuth will try and see what I can find out. Look, don't worry. I'm sure you're not in any danger."

"It's not me I'm worried about. It's Brace, and how can you be sure?"

A pause. "You're right, I can't. But it sounds too outlandish. Who'd want to hurt a guide dog?"

"Who'd want to steal cats, except one of those awful research labs? You know that Boomer's missing."

"Yeah. I was part of the search effort. Is that what Meg thinks? That some thug stole him to sell to a lab?"

"Yes, because she's pretty sure that's what Dr. Reynolds thinks."

There was a silence during which Pip made a turn.

"This isn't the way home," I said, knowing by heart all the turns leading to Aunt Marion's house.

"I'm taking you on a short extra drive because we're in the middle of talking. Okay?"

"Okay. Sorry. Guess I'm getting paranoid!"

"You are. But I don't blame you."

"And there was the man in the car that nearly ran over Brace and me a couple of days ago. He didn't say anything, but there was this screech of tires again, and I could feel the wind as he went by. Funny, until just now I hadn't thought of it again."

"Jocelyn, there are dumb bastards who drive like maniacs and don't give a damn for children or animals or old people. What you're talking about now could easily be one of those. I'm not belittling what happened just now or in the tape shop, but you have to keep a balance or you'll confuse what's dumb but nothing special from what's something else."

"All right. And then there's Sandy Martin." Her unprovoked nastiness had upset me more than I realized.

"What about Sandy Martin?" Was Pip's voice a little sharper?

I told him about the two occasions and her seemingly motiveless rudeness. "I can't think why she's doing this! I never even heard of her before. Has she been at school long?"

"How would I know?" Pip said.

We'd always been absolutely honest. That was why our relationship was so good and worked so well. On the other hand, to repeat what Meg had said, about Sandy's being one of Pip's ex-girlfriends, would go into territory that we'd always kept out of. "Well, would you?" I asked. "I mean, would you know if she'd been at school long?"

There was a pause while the car turned again. Then Pip said, "She's been at school just a few weeks. Said she'd come to Brinton from Meridan to live with her uncle because her parents were getting a divorce and she didn't want to stick around."

Hadn't Meg said something about Pip getting it on with a girl from Meridan? The effort not to say something like "Then Meg was right. You do know her" was overwhelming. It was as though I were leaning against a door, keeping the words out.

"Okay," Pip said, as though I had spoken the words aloud. "I know her, as I'm sure a whole bunch of your friends would be the first to tell you. I . . . she . . . not that it's any of your business!"

"I never said, or implied, it was. Just let Brace and me out. We can walk the rest of the way!"

"For pete's sake! You don't even know where you are. Leave the door alone. I'll take you home. If that's what you want!"

"That's what you said you were going to do."

"I also said we were going to take a slight detour so we could chat! What a great idea that turned out to be!"

"What are you so angry about? What have I said? And where are we, anyway?"

"We are now in front of your house, or will be in less than a minute. Okay. Here we are. Don't let me keep you!"

To my astonishment, he leaned across me and pushed open the door. "You can let Brace out yourself!"

I got out as quickly as I could and then opened the door for Brace. "Come along, Brace. We're home." I took hold of his harness with my left hand and we started up the path.

I knew Pip hadn't driven off. Part of me was furious at the squall that had suddenly blown up. Part of me wanted desperately for him to call me back, to say something that would undo everything that had just happened. But he didn't do that. As Brace and I reached the front door, I heard him leave.

"Was that Pip?" Aunt Marion called through the door of her study as Brace and I came through the front hall.

"Yes."

"Come in here a moment, Jocelyn. I'd like to talk to you."

My heart sank. People almost never say that when they want to tell you you've won the lottery or been chosen the outstanding person of all time by public poll. Brace and I went in. If it had been my own room or a part of the house that was fairly unchanging, such as the kitchen or living room, I'd have put him on a lead instead of the harness. But with Aunt Marion's study, I'd learned the hard way you never knew what piece of furniture or pile of books might just have been put in the middle of the floor.

"Okay," I said, when we were in front of her desk. "What?"

"Why don't you sit down? There's a chair just behind you."

I felt back with my right hand, located an armchair, and lowered myself into it.

Aunt Marion cleared her throat. "I've known the Mowbrays for years. Pip's parents are nominally members of Saint James. Though of course they never show up. . . ." She stopped, then went on. "Maybe if you weren't — er — handicapped, I wouldn't be saying all this. After all, you're almost an adult. But you are, and I guess that increases my sense of responsibility. . . ."

"What is it, Aunt Marion?" I hadn't meant to sound sharp, but I knew I did.

"Just that Pip is known as a wild boy, and somehow lately it seems to have gotten worse. I know that boys his age can hardly be held to the kind of sober behavior that their fathers have —"

"Maybe if his father liked him he'd wouldn't be tearing around the way he does."

"That may be true, but —"

"And his mother's a drunk!"

"Are you — er — serious about him, Jocelyn? The way you leap to his defense you sound as though you are."

"That's stupid. We're just friends. But I don't like to hear my friends criticized."

"If you're just friends, then why are you reacting the way you are?"

"If you said that about Meg I'd feel the same."

"No, I don't think you would — at least it wouldn't sound quite the same. But your defensiveness makes me even more certain than I was that I should be warning you. I've been thinking about it for weeks. Now I wish I'd spoken sooner."

I got up. "I told you. Pip and I are just friends. Who he goes out with and what he does with them is none of my business."

"It's your business if he's sleeping with every girl that comes his way."

"You don't know that," I said furiously. "That's just gossip among a lot of old women who have nothing better to do than run the church and whisper about anybody who's young and having — having a good time!"

"I've never been a moralistic prig, Jocelyn! If you don't believe me about Pip, ask some of your friends!"

"I won't listen to you!" I got up, fumbled for Brace's harness and walked out.

"Jocelyn!" But I almost ran into the hall and up the stairs to my room. Once there I slammed the door and then took Brace's harness and lead off.

"It's not true!" I said angrily to Brace. But I knew it almost certainly was. Meg had said as much about Pip, and I'd heard before what other kids had said. But all that had never bothered me. Why did it bother me now?

I sat on my bed, my hands on my knees. Suddenly, and for the second time in a few days, I felt the tears coming down my cheeks. I groped in my jeans pocket for some tissue, then felt Brace's nose push against my knee.

Finally I lay down on the bed, and Brace, who usually sleeps on the floor beside me, lay down on the bed next to me. My right arm was under my head. I crossed my left hand over my body to rub his head.

There was a soft growl, and I heard Cyrus jump from the window onto the floor. A half minute later, he was on top of me, his purr rattling through both of us. And in the midst of my misery I wondered how Aunt Marion could persist in her lack of affection for animals. They were so much nicer than people, I thought, even Pip.

Then, as I lay there, I knew Aunt Marion was right: I was in love with Pip. What was it Meg had said about being in love? "It's like being in heaven and wanting to die at the same time."

But for me it wasn't like that. It was like a huge ache, a certainty that whatever it was I wanted — when it depended on other people, like now — I wouldn't get. It was a feeling related to the knowledge I'd had since the accident: that so much of life would never be for me. Where I got the feeling

I didn't know. From the first hospital on, people had stressed again and again that in most ways I could have a normal life. But I knew now I never believed them. Not really.

Slowly I sat up.

"Come on, Brace, we have to go down and practice the piano."

Jeremy would be here later this afternoon and I had not been practicing as faithfully as I should have, or as I usually did. That's what I should be doing, I thought as I got up. Serious piano work was a possibility for me. It was something I could do myself — I didn't have to depend on what somebody else felt about me. Going after things I couldn't have was stupid. Like mooning over Pip.

I worked for an hour on the first movement of the Schumann concerto, touching the braille notes, first with the right hand as I played the bass with the left, and then playing the treble with my right hand, reading the braille with my left. After a while I could work from memory with both hands together.

Jeremy came in as I was finishing.

"That's good," he said, "considering I only gave you this last week. You must have been working hard."

For a moment I let myself bask in the praise. Then I said, "Not as hard as I should. I've really only been working hard on it today."

"Well, that's honest of you." I heard him bring up his usual chair.

"Shall I go back to the beginning?"

"Yes."

So I went back to the beginning and played through it again. Somewhat to my surprise Jeremy didn't stop me, the way he usually does when I'm beginning a new piece. When I had stumbled through it he said, "It's going to need a lot of work, Jocelyn, not just spot work here and there. But if you're willing to invest your time and effort in it — you have the talent, or I wouldn't be saying this — then I think you could go far."

"What do you mean by far?"

"That'll depend upon you."

"All right. But do you mean, maybe I could get into Juilliard if I applied and become a teacher, or do you mean — possibly — concert work?" I'd never said the words, even to myself.

"To quote a teacher of mine once, to become a top-rate concert pianist you have to be a genius among geniuses, and to start early."

"Earlier than I have?"

"Jocelyn — don't push me. I don't know how far you can go. And it's no use pretending you don't have a handicap. But, strictly speaking, it shouldn't affect your technique. All I can do is help you with that. It's up to you. Now let's go back to the opening."

We worked for another hour. But the awful part was, while I was working at the notes and technique and listening to Jeremy, I was also listening for another sound — the sound of the phone, or maybe of Pip's car.

"You're not concentrating," Jeremy said.

"Sorry. I'll try and do better." And I did, forcing myself to listen only to the music itself.

When I'd finished Jeremy said, "That's more like it." I heard him push back the chair. "Work on the opening, Jocelyn." He walked across and put the chair back where it had been. Then he stopped. "I hadn't really intended to say this today, but — well, why not? There's going to be a recital in the school auditorium in about three or four months. Another teacher and I are having one or two of our best students play. If you can work on the Schumann so you can be ready for that, I'd like you to play. But you're really going to have to work. Okay?"

"I can't do it!"

"If you say you can't, then you can't. But if I didn't think it was possible for you, I wouldn't ask you. Here." I heard him put something down on the piano. "That's a tape of the orchestra part. After you've worked on the piano for a while you can practice with that."

Two days later it was my evening for helping feed the homeless. The meals were offered four times a week, but most volunteers worked only one day a week at the most.

"Come along, Brace," I said. "Let's go to the parish house."

As we walked, my mind kept returning to what Jeremy had said — to his belief that I could play at the recital, to my hope that he was right and fear that he wasn't. And, behind it all, I was still listening for Pip's car. I knew that if he came up now I'd accept a ride, even though I also knew it would be stupid. Why torture myself, like Meg? I'd listened to Meg and her obsessive self-doubts about her weight and her freckles with what I knew now was a superior attitude, as though I were immune. "You're probably just oversensitive," I said once, in my role as Ms. Above-It-All. I knew I was thin, or in the flattering words of one girl, slim. Until this moment I hadn't realized how much comfort that had given me. I had never felt rejected for the way I looked. People went out of their way to tell me I was pretty, to make up for the fact that I couldn't look in the mirror and see for myself.

But Meg had moaned and groaned about her defects. "I can't even try to get tan," she said. "First I come out in blisters and then I'm wall-to-wall freckles."

41

"Don't they have special tanning stuff — strong protection and all that jazz?"

"Not for me. I've talked to Mr. Rosen down at the drugstore till I was blue in the face. But after the last full-strength stuff didn't work, leaving me with more freckles than ever, I've given up. And besides all that, it's not as though I were a dream of beauty in a bathing suit. My tummy sticks out and my thighs are fat. If only I could just find the right diet and stay on it!"

I was thin and I didn't have freckles, but I knew now how she felt.

Pip didn't stop to give me a lift, so ten minutes later Brace and I arrived at the parish hall.

Mrs. Brent and I have worked out the best way for me to cope when I'm there. I usually stand at the kitchen table behind a dish of something that can be served with a big spoon or scoop or dispenser. Whoever's standing next to me can keep an eye on the food I'm putting on people's plates, to make sure I haven't failed to scoop it up, whatever it is — rice, mashed potatoes, or vegetables. And, of course, I feel the position of the plate with my other hand. Occasionally I'll miss getting the food into the spoon properly, at which point the other server is supposed to tell me, but, as Mrs. Brent told Aunt Marion, those being served are as quick to point it out as anyone. Brace, off his harness, usually sits in one corner of the big kitchen, and a lot of old-timers among the homeless greet him along with me.

I've always felt perfectly safe in having Brace there. Today, I knew I was anxious about him. There was no way I could have him at my feet, because the various kitchen workers passing large pots and hot serving dishes back and forth would trip over him. So I put him in the same place as always, but every few minutes I asked whoever was standing near me if Brace was okay.

"That's the third time you've asked that in an hour," one of the volunteers said. "Are you worried about something?"

I had to say something. I couldn't just say "no," and leave it at that. "Animals have disappeared," I said.

I was expecting her to think I was crazy. But instead she said, "I know. A couple of people's pets have vanished. They're out of their minds with worry." She paused, and I heard her plonk some of the food she was dispensing onto somebody's plate. "Jeremy Stoddard's English bulldog is one of those that's disappeared. He's had that dog since it was two months old. It's a shame!"

"**H**i, Jocelyn!"

It was Danny, one of the homeless.

I could tell by his voice that he was young, and others had told me that he was probably a schizophrenic. He was also an animal lover and a great admirer of Brace, and we had talked on the subject once or twice. I knew he fed stray cats. Where he slept, no one knew.

"Hi, Danny! Want some potatoes?"

"Yes. Brace is looking real well."

"Yes, he is. But —"

"You holdin' up the line?" the man behind Danny said indignantly. "I'm hungry if you're not."

"I'll talk to you later, Danny," I said. "I have to concentrate."

I kept on dishing out the food, feeling with my hand for the plate in front of me and with my spoon for how empty the serving dish was getting and estimating how soon I'd need to call for more potatoes. I was upset about Jeremy Stoddard's dog, General. I knew how Jeremy felt about him. Occasionally Jeremy brought him over when he gave me a lesson and I loved to feel his squashed-in face.

As soon as my part of the serving was over I collected Brace, put his harness on and slid out of the big downstairs dining room to a telephone booth upstairs. From there I called Jeremy. But he was either out or giving a lesson at home, during which, I knew, he didn't answer the phone. I left a message on his tape about how sorry I was about General, then went downstairs again to see if I could start loading the dishwasher.

"Jocelyn?" Danny's voice was just behind me as I was going into the kitchen.

"Yes, Danny."

"Look, one of the cats I look after just had kittens. Do you think you could take a couple?"

I stopped. After a minute, I said, "The trouble is, Danny, because I'm blind I could easily step on one of the kittens and either kill it or injure it badly."

"Yeah, I can understand that. But — isn't there a room you could put them in?"

I thought about Aunt Marion, who would almost certainly be less than welcoming to new kittens. There were three bedrooms upstairs. Aunt Marion had the master bedroom. I had the next biggest one. And then there was the guest room. We didn't often have guests, but I knew Aunt Marion liked to be able to offer people hospitality. However, it was sometimes a year between visits.

"Trouble is, Jocelyn," Danny said, "if you don't take them, they're pretty sure to die. There are raccoons near where I am. And the mother's got to leave them to find food sometime."

"What about the animal shelter?"

"That's in the town. I don't like to go there."

I knew that Danny lived in mortal fear that somebody would snatch him up and put him in the hospital. It had happened before. And while I thought he ought to be in a hospital where he could get treatment and medicine, I also knew I couldn't be part of a plan to force him there.

"Okay," I said. "How old are they now?"

45

"About eight weeks." He paused. "Big enough to run around and get eaten."

"All right," I said. I'd worry about Aunt Marion later. I was about to go back into the kitchen when Danny said, "I don't mean to get you upset. But I think you oughta —" He stopped and giggled suddenly in a way he had. "I was gonna say keep an eye on — only that's not possible, is it? — anyway, watch Brace. I mean, know where he is all the time."

That fright I'd felt before gripped me again. Was he talking about the man in the video store and the car? If so, how did he know about him? "What do you mean?" I asked sharply. Without even thinking I put my right hand on Brace's head, touching it, reassuring myself.

I could hear Danny edge off, shuffling near the stairs that led up to the ground floor. "Nothing special. Just watch him. I'll bring the kittens here tomorrow just before the feeding. 'Bye." And he was gone. One minute he was there and the next minute he wasn't.

"I know Danny's a friend of yours," Mrs. Brent said, coming from the direction of the dining room. "But I wish he'd take a bath. I feel sorry for him, and for his family, wherever they are, but he stinks, literally, he really does."

"Yes, I know."

"Did he say something to disturb you?" she said abruptly.

"Why?" I asked, not wanting to answer right away.

"You look upset."

I didn't want to go into my fears about Brace and the man in the store and the car, but to repeat what Danny had said without explaining that would make him sound even nuttier than usual. And after all, he'd been trying to do me a favor.

"I just wish he'd go to the hospital and let them treat him," I said.

"He's been in the hospital, several times," Mrs. Brent said.

"Did they mistreat him?"

"I don't think so, but I don't know. He once let out that he has a perfectly ordinary middle-class family somewhere. I bet they'd like him to get treatment." She sighed. "But, of course, if he doesn't want it, they can't force him."

I shrugged. "What would you like me to do next?" I had a firm hold of the harness. Through it I could feel Brace's movement and knew for the moment he was safe.

"If you could help load the second dishwasher —"

"All right."

The next day at class I told Meg about the kitten and about what Danny had said.

"Did you hear about Jeremy Stoddard's dog?" she said gloomily. "He was one of Daddy's patients. Daddy says Jeremy's almost beside himself."

"Yes, I heard. Hasn't anyone seen the dog?"

"No more than they've seen Boomer."

"Meg, I'm scared. What's going on?"

"I don't know. Daddy doesn't know, and he says the police don't know, because he's been in touch with them. But there's a bunch of new kids in town. You can see them around the mall and video stores especially. I bet that kid in the tape store you told me about was one of them, also the one that yelled at you from the car about Brace. What did he say?"

I told her. "And you've got to be right about his being from out of town. I can't imagine anyone in the town here saying anything like that. Pip said —" I stopped as pain at the mention of his name went through me.

"Pip said what?"

I took a breath. "That he'd ask one of the kids who works there if he knew who the jerk was."

"Maybe he will. I still bet it's one of those new kids. I've seen them in the mall. Nobody knows who they are or where they come from."

"Couldn't the police find out?"

"I think they've tried, at least according to what they told Dad. But they haven't gotten anywhere. The kids haven't actually done anything — not that the police know, anyway. They just roll into town, swagger around the mall and entertainment area and then split. Talk about weird!"

"Nobody's seen them with any animals?"

"Absolutely not. In fact, the police don't think it's they who've taken the animals."

"Who do they think have done it?"

"They just say they have other leads. I hope . . . I just hope whoever has Boomer isn't hurting him."

I reached out and took her hand.

That afternoon I got over to the parish house before the feeding was due to begin. Danny was waiting for me.

"Hi!" he said as I walked up. "Here they are. I've put them in a box so you can carry them. They eat anything." And he reached out, took my hand and slid the string tying the box over my fingers.

I could feel the box bouncing around.

"The one that's a little bigger, he's the male. He's all black. The other one is female. She's tiger-striped gray and black. Listen, thanks a lot." And he slid away almost noiselessly.

"All right, Brace, let's go," I said. "And let's be careful!"

The church and parish house were on the main road leading into town and I could hear cars swishing past in both directions. Since I've had Brace I've never been afraid of cars and traffic. Nor have I been afraid for myself. Brinton is a small town and all the townspeople I've had anything to do with have been decent and kind. But now I realized I was walking faster than usual; I knew that my encounters in both the tape shop and the road had damaged my sense of security.

I heard a car slow down and stiffened. It was on my side of the road. Straining my ears, I tried to hear if there were any other feet walking near me, any voices.

"There's that terrific dog again," the same voice as before came at me. "And what's that in your hand? More wildlife?"

I fought down a sense of panic at my own vulnerability and my utter uselessness in defending either Brace or the kittens.

"Go away!" I heard my own voice, loud and angry, and prayed that somebody else would hear it, too.

"Now is that any way to talk to an animal lover?"

I heard the car door open somewhere to my side.

"Right, Brace," I said, and, with the box in my hand, tried to make the classic hand signal to turn right. I had no idea what I'd be turning into, but I hoped it was somebody's lawn and somebody's house where I could go up and ring the bell. After all, it would take a hard person to stand by and see a blind person abused and robbed — or so I told myself.

"Not so fast," the same voice, now ugly and sadistic, came towards me.

Then I heard another voice — Pip's — yell, "Who the hell —" followed by a funny-sounding crack, the noise of another car door slamming and a screech of brakes.

"Are you okay, Joss? It's me, Pip."

"Yes, I'm fine. Thanks, oh, thanks!"

I heard him come over. Then I felt his hands on my shoulders. "Come on," he said. "Let me take you home."

He led me to his car, opened the door, put me and the box of kittens in, then opened the back door for Brace.

"Pip, did you see him? That was the one who spoke to me from the car the other day, the one who had the 'aboot the hoose' kind of accent —"

"Yeah, I saw him. And I've seen him around somewhere, although I can't be sure where. What else did he say to you?"

"Just something about there's that great or terrific dog again, and something about more wildlife. I guess he saw the box moving."

"I take it that's a kitten or puppy?"

"Two kittens. Danny gave them to me."

"Who's Danny?"

I tried desperately to think that his voice might have sharpened with the question, as in being jealous, but I couldn't kid myself. Pip sounded perfectly normal.

"Danny's one of the homeless who gets fed at Saint James. Mrs. Brent says he's a schizophrenic, and he does sound strange, sometimes. But he takes care of a cat wherever it is he sleeps. Only she's had kittens, and he says there's a raccoon in the park and he's afraid that they might be killed. So I said I'd take two."

"How's the reverend going to like that? She's never impressed me as being sentimental about animals."

"She isn't. I'm not even sure she likes Brace. But what else could I do? I sort of hoped if I got them to the guest room she mightn't notice."

There was a short silence. Then Pip said, "If she gives you flak, tell her you're keeping them for me and that I promised to take them."

"Thanks, Pip." I opened the box and put my hand in and encountered two warm, wiggling furry bodies that promptly tried to climb up out of the box.

"They're cute," Pip said.

"Danny said one was black and the other striped gray and black."

"That's right." His hand came and joined mine in the box. He squeezed mine and then withdrew his. "I'm sorry about the other day," he said. "I don't know how to explain it, exactly. What with one thing and another — and especially if I've been drinking — I've been doing things lately that I'm not especially proud of. The whole thing about . . . about Sandy was one. I guess that's why I was feeling defensive."

I knew it was insane for me to feel as wildly happy as I did at that moment. It didn't really mean anything, I told myself. But I guess I didn't believe it, because the happiness was like flying. "I'm sorry, too, for being rude." Without any wishing it on my part my left hand went out and I touched his arm.

"Pax," he said, taking my hand in his.

"Pax," I repeated.

After a minute he said, "Where're you going to keep the kittens?"

"In the spare bedroom, I think. I'd take them into mine, but I don't know how Cyrus will feel about it, and I don't think they ought to be running around where I can fall over them."

"Would you fall over them less in the spare bedroom?"

"I don't know. I worry about it."

"You could hurt yourself."

"I could kill one of the kittens if I stepped on it."

"How do you plan to manage, then?"

"I guess just sliding my feet along the floor and not making any sudden moves."

"It sounds to me like an invitation to disaster!"

"Don't say that, Pip! I mean — I'm sorry, I didn't mean to snap. It's just that it's important for me not to be afraid.

51

People mean well, but they run around doing things for me and it drives me bananas sometimes. One reason why I've always" — to my horror I realized I was going to say "loved" — "liked you," I said, rushing on, "was that you didn't do that."

"What did you almost say?" he asked.

"Nothing," I said, and then repeated, "Nothing."

"Okay. Do it your way. But my offer still stands — about taking the kittens. And if you think I can't be trusted with them, I'll give them to Jack Carter, who lives over the stable. He loves animals and already has about three cats."

"Thanks, Pip. Thanks a lot. Are we home?"

"Yes. Come on, I'll help you with the kittens."

Considering what Aunt Marion had said about him, I wasn't sure his arriving with the kittens would make her like the idea any better, but I wasn't going to refuse. And anyway, she might be out.

"Did you hear?" I said. "Jeremy's bulldog is missing, as well as Meg's Boomer?"

"That's too bad. I wonder if there is a connection between that and the new kids who seem to be all over."

"I thought there was, but Meg said her father talked to the police and they didn't think so. He said they had other leads."

"Umm. Here we are. Do you have a key or do we ring the bell?"

"I have a key." I felt in my pocket and got it out. Putting my hand on the door, I felt for the lock and inserted the key and then pushed the door open. "Would you like to come in?"

"Thanks, but I've already cut half of swimming practice. If I cut the other half I'll be in real trouble. Is your aunt home?"

I stood for a moment in the hall, listening. "I don't think

so," I said. Nineteen out of twenty times I was right about whether the house was empty.

"Okay. Here are the baby lions. Have fun, all of you." I felt his hand against my face, and then the door closed.

"Brace," I whispered. "Do you think he — he cares for me?" I couldn't quite bring myself to say the word *love*, not even when I was talking to Brace.

Through the harness I could feel Brace move slightly.

"Good dog!" I said, and then stood there, thinking. The matter of the kittens would need some organizing.

Putting the box down and letting Brace out of the harness, I went into the kitchen. Feeling my way, I collected some plastic bags and poured some milk into one of Cyrus's bowls, silently asking his forgiveness. Then, followed by Brace, I picked up the box, went upstairs and put all the items down on the floor in the spare bedroom. After that, I went into my own room.

"Cy!" He usually was asleep in the middle of my bed at this time of day. And he always responded to my voice. But there was no cushiony meow.

"Cy!" I said again and then stood still. Brace had come into the room with me, of course. I stood there, with my hand on his head, but I knew that Cyrus wasn't there. Maybe he's out hunting, I told myself. I collected a can of his food and another dish, then picked up his bag of kitty litter and went back to the spare bedroom, shutting the door behind me. The box was now jumping around on the floor. The poor kittens must be frantic, I thought. Fighting with the string, I got it off and opened the box. The little furry bodies swarmed over my hand and onto the floor, mewing and squeaking. I lined the cardboard box, now empty, with one of the plastic bags. Then, picking up the litter bag, I poured some litter on top of the plastic lining of the box.

There was no mewing now, just lapping, as they found

the bowl of milk. Using the pull-tab on top of the can of food I opened it, emptied the food into the dish and put the dish down. Instantly I felt a nose pressed against my hand and a tongue trying to reach the food. I felt both kittens, and decided that the aggressive one was the small female described by Danny as tiger-striped. I thought I'd call her Danielle and her brother Danny, after their rescuer. For a moment I sat there on the floor, wondering if it wouldn't be easier simply to take them into my room, but that meant Cyrus would have no place to hide from them, and I decided it would be better to introduce him to them a bit at a time.

I sat back against the bed in the spare bedroom and listened to the industrious sounds of eating. Brace was sprawled out beside me.

I must have dozed off, because I awoke hearing Aunt Marion's voice. "Jocelyn? Jocelyn? Are you upstairs?"

I was about to get quickly to my feet when I remembered the kittens. At the same moment I became aware that something warm was lying on my thigh. One of the kittens was asleep there, and, moving my foot, I discovered the other was on the floor beside it. Putting the one that had been on my leg next to the other, I stood up and slid to the door as fast as I could. Then I opened it as narrowly as possible and slipped out, letting Brace out right after me. Praying that neither of the kittens had waked up enough to follow me into the hall, I called down, "Aunt Marion, I'm here."

"Oh! I went up to your room but you weren't there, so I came down again."

"I . . ." I took a deep breath. Not to tell Aunt Marion about the kittens would almost ensure that that would be the one day that she'd go into the spare bedroom for some reason. "I was in the spare bedroom, Aunt Marion. We — we have some guests."

"Oh, who?" I heard her start up the stairs.

"Two kittens," I said. "Danielle and Danny. They'd have been eaten by a raccoon if I hadn't taken them." Desperate at the ensuing silence, I rushed on, "And I promise to keep them up here where they won't bother your allergy."

By this time Aunt Marion was back up the stairs. I heard her sigh. "Where on earth did you get them?"

"From Danny — you know, one of the homeless. It was the cat he looks after that had the kittens."

"Well, speaking of Danny, the reason I was calling you was that the police station was on the phone. It seems that they've arrested Danny and he has asked for you in place of a relative or a lawyer. I didn't think you ought to go down there and get mixed up in this, so I told them I'd give you the message but — where are you going?"

"To see Danny. Please don't throw the kittens out, Aunt Marion. If you're really afraid to have them in the house, I'll find another home for them as soon as I get back. Come on, Brace!" I was already struggling with his harness.

"Of course I won't, Jocelyn!" she said rather indignantly.

But Brace and I were already down the stairs and out the front door.

SEVEN

"What's Danny done?" I asked the detective to whom I had been taken.

"He's being held on suspicion of kidnapping," the detective said. "And we'd like very much to know what you know about it."

"Danny! He'd never do a thing like that!"

"No? What makes you so sure? He's a crazy who lives in the park and steals food from the local market when he thinks he can get away with it."

"I bet you anything he doesn't. I know he begs, but that's not the same thing."

"One of the grocers in the area said he did, and I'd take his word before I would that of a homeless weirdo."

"Can I speak to him now?"

"How old are you?"

"Seventeen. Why?"

"Does your aunt know you hobnob with somebody like Danny?"

"Since she was the one you talked to and since she gave me your message, she must, mustn't she?"

"And she knows and approves your coming here?"

"Yes," I said, remembering clearly that Aunt Marion was still protesting my coming down to the jail when I left.

"Of course I can always call her and check," he said, his hand on the phone.

Two or three snappy answers were on the tip of my tongue. But I suddenly recalled I was here to help Danny. "Why do you think he's involved in kidnapping? The only animal he has is the cat in the park who's a stray. And he gave me two of the kittens she just had."

"Cat? Kittens? What are you talking about?"

I was about to tell him about Boomer and Jeremy Stoddard's General when I thought he might blame that on Danny, too. "Nothing. What kidnapping do you think Danny might be involved in?"

"I think you were about to say something else when you thought better of it. What was it?"

"Nothing," I said again. "Can I see Danny?"

"All in good time. I want to know what it was you didn't say."

"If he asked for me, aren't you supposed to let me see him?"

"Only if you're his lawyer or a near relative. Are you either of these?"

"No, but he did ask for me."

"Yes, I know, and I'd like to know why." He paused, and then said, "Smelling the way he does, I'm surprised any nicely brought-up girl would want to have anything to do with him."

I was afraid anything I said could be used against Danny as part of his craziness so he could be hauled off to the hospital. I stood there, unable to think of a thing to say. Finally I said, "Right about face, Brace. We have to go see a lawyer."

"Whoa," the detective said. "What lawyer?"

"I don't believe I have to tell you that, but I will. Nathaniel Mowbray."

Until that moment calling Pip's father had never entered my mind. I had no intention now of doing it, but his name in Brinton was a prominent one.

"All right," the detective said. "You can see Danny, but if your aunt objects — and she'd be crazy if she didn't — I have several witnesses here who'll testify that you threatened to go to a lawyer. Gene, take Joss — er — Miss Hunter down to see Danny."

"Thanks," I said.

"You want to hang on to my arm?" asked the policeman who came up.

"Yes." I let Brace's harness go and picked up his leash instead. "Do you know what kidnapping Danny's suspected of?"

"Well, I guess I shouldn't mention it, since Sergeant Ferrarro didn't tell you."

"I don't want to get you into trouble. But —" Again I almost mentioned Boomer and General. And again I was afraid that he'd tell the horrible detective and they'd accuse Danny of it.

"But what?"

"Nothing," I repeated, feeling stupid and incompetent.

We got to the bottom of the steps and the cop led me through a door. "Danny, here's your friend. You don't have too much time — about ten minutes." He said to me, "I'll come back for you."

"Hi, Danny," I said, and put my hand through the bars.

"Hi, Jocelyn." He waited a minute and then said in a low voice, "I want to make sure he's not listening, although I suppose they have bugs everywhere."

"Why would they want to have bugs?"

"All government people bug everything. Didn't you know that?"

"Danny, I don't think that's true."

"I know it's true. It's a national conspiracy and I —"

I recognized the beginning of Danny's favorite world plot theory. "Danny, why did you want to see me?"

Pause. "Would you find my cat and feed her? She'll starve if I don't get back soon. Or some of the creeps who are stealing the other animals will take her. Please!"

"Of course. But how do I find her?"

"You know where that big rock is in the higher section of the park?"

"Yes. There's a plaque on it, isn't there, with the name on it of the man who started the park? I remember feeling it."

"Yeah. I think so. Anyway, on one side there's a sort of low shelf. I feed Cat there. So if you go there just call out, 'Cat, Cat,' the way I do, and wait a few minutes. She'll come running."

"Is that where you live?"

"Sort of. Not far from there."

I could hear the evasion in his voice, and his feet start to slide around the way they always did when he didn't want to talk or answer questions. "Okay. Sure, I'll go there, with some food." I thought for a moment. "Does she have a place to go where she'll be safe, in case those monsters come looking for her?"

"Yeah. She'll be okay, if she can just get food. 'Course she can hunt, but that brings her out in the open."

"Danny — tell me what you know about Boomer and General."

"Those are Dr. Reynolds's daughter's cat and the organist's dog, aren't they?"

"Yes. How did you know about them?"

I could hear his feet skittering around. "I hear things."

"Please, please tell me. Meg is out of her mind with worry, and Jeremy is just as upset. Who are they, the ones doing these things?"

"I dunno," he mumbled. I was pretty sure he was lying. "Will ya go and feed Cat?"

"All right, I will, if you tell me about those people."

"If you tell anybody I said anything, Jocelyn, they'll come after me. I know it. And they'll get Cat."

"I won't," I said. "At least not unless that's the only way they can be rescued. Please!"

"I don't know much. Just that they talk about liberating the animals. At least that's what the person who told me said. He said he'd heard them at night when they come in in their cars and park them near the mall. He hangs out there and hears a lot. He also says they talk funny — I mean, they say words that don't make any sense to him."

"What kind of words?"

"I dunno. He said he'd never heard them before."

"Foreign language?"

"Maybe. He didn't say that. Anyhow, how'd he know a foreign language?"

"Would you?"

"Depends on what it is. Now promise you'll feed Cat!"

"I've already said I would!" Suddenly I got a new idea. "If the detective doesn't know about the animals — and I don't think he does — what are you here for?"

"He keeps asking me about a Barbara something. Says I was seen hanging around the last place she was seen. Jocelyn, I swear I never even heard of her. You know how I live. I don't even like going anywhere near the middle of town. I —"

"Barbara Weldon?" I interrupted. "Is that the name he used?"

"Yeah, I think so. Do you know about her? Who is she?"

"She's a kid at school who suddenly disappeared. You're sure you don't know her?"

It was stupid and unkind of me to ask. I'd forgotten how crazy Danny could be. He started jumping around. "Jocelyn, I never heard of her! I don't know nothing about her. All I care about is Cat and other animals. You know that. That's why I asked you to come. You know that!"

I could hear his rising hysteria. "Danny! I'm sorry! Ssh! Of course I'll take care of Cat. Don't worry about it. And I won't tell anyone what you said."

"You won't tell anyone what?" It was the voice of Ferrarro, the detective, behind me.

"I won't tell anyone how Danny feeds some of the stray animals."

"Why not?" His voice was sharp. On the other side of the bars I could hear Danny almost crying.

"Because then some wicked people might be tempted to throw out their pets if they get inconvenient."

"I think you're feeding me a lot of — garbage," he said.

"No, I'm not." I took hold of Brace's harness. "Now I'm going to call Mr. Mowbray."

"And who's going to pay for that?"

"He does a lot of pro bono work, didn't you know that, Detective?"

"So?" But his tone accepted what I said. Maybe Pip's father would help Danny. I'd ask Pip, I thought — and hoped violently that I wasn't just thinking up an excuse to call him. "Good-bye, Danny. I'll look after that matter. Don't worry about it." I said. "Forward, Brace."

"How're you going to get home?" the detective asked, as I got upstairs.

"The same way I got here. Walking."

"I can arrange to have you driven home, if you like."

"Thanks, but Brace and I need the exercise." I also didn't

want to accept any favors from the police, not if they were out to get Danny.

The police station is in the center of town, so home was a little more than a mile away through our business section and along well-populated streets. I was glad Brace and I were going to be walking among a lot of people, and that was an indication of how much the episodes involving voices coming from cars or cars stopping hovered in my mind. Normally I prefer country roads where the smells are more those of grass and flowers than exhaust fumes and the sounds are those of birds rather than cars. Thinking about that, I felt my anger against the strangers growing. Not only were they threatening people's pets, they were destroying my independence, which depended on my being unafraid.

Brace and I had been walking briskly when I felt him stop at a curb. That meant we had to wait for a light. Cars went by. Then one stopped near me. The voice came out of nowhere.

"I still think it's a pity that dog has to be cooped up in that harness. Why don't you let him go?" The voice was a little to my left and behind me, so the car was on the road at right angles to the one I was waiting to cross. I turned.

"Go for what?"

"For a different life." He laughed. "A higher life."

"What are you talking about?"

"Join us and find out!"

"You're crazy! Do you make a practice of harassing blind people?" I asked.

"Only when they inflict their handicap on animals."

"I don't inflict my handicap on anyone. You're the one who's inflicting your craziness on people's pets."

"Only so they can serve a higher purpose."

"What are you talking about?" I heard him laugh again.

"You're from Virginia, aren't you?" I said. "I wonder what the police can find out about stolen animals there?"

His voice changed. He snarled, "You better watch what you say, blind girl!"

I heard and felt the car roar near and threw myself around Brace. There was the same screeching sound I'd heard before as it went off into the distance.

I was shaking, and when I put my hands on Brace, I could feel him trembling. "It's all right, Brace," I whispered. But I knew that I didn't believe that myself. It wasn't all right. I straightened and stood quite still for a moment. Cars were passing swiftly, going both ways in front of me. If the light had changed, it had obviously changed back. I couldn't feel that anybody was around me. But I thought I'd make sure. "Is anyone here with me at the light?" I asked. There was no reply. I felt exposed and afraid and angry. I wished now that I had accepted the detective's offer of a ride home. But it was too late. And for Pip to appear suddenly again was too much to hope for.

Brace and I went the rest of the way home. Every time a car stopped near me I fought a tendency to jump. When I reached home I stood still for a moment, trying to hear whether Aunt Marion was in. If she were, I'd go straight to my room and use the telephone there. But the house felt empty. Just to make sure I called out, "Aunt Marion? You home?" Silence. I called again. Still no reply. Then I remembered that she might be celebrating Evensong this evening.

Releasing Brace, I went into the living room, picked up the phone and dialed Pip's number. To my great relief he answered.

"Pip, it's me, Jocelyn."

"Let me pick myself off the floor, Joss. You calling me?"

"Don't joke. I think I need your father."

His voice lost some of its lightness. "I could do with a little of his attention myself. Why do you want him?"

"The police have Danny in jail. They claim he knows something about Barbara Weldon's disappearance. Pip, you know he wouldn't do anything like that."

"You're the one who knows him, not me, but if you say he wouldn't, I'll take your word for it. Where does my esteemed father come into this?"

"I told the police Danny should have a lawyer, and the only one whose name I could remember was your father. I told them he did a lot of pro bono work."

"Oh, he does, he does. He bleeds for the poor and outcast. Has lots more time for them than he does for his children. Besides, it brings him good publicity. Rich lawyer donates time and effort to society's outcasts." There was a bitter note in Pip's voice. "Anyway, Dad took off for Tokyo, Hong Kong, and parts east two days ago."

"Oh."

"I'd talk to the one guy in his office that has a friendly word to say to me, but unfortunately, he's with the old man."

"Do you know any other lawyers who might help Danny for nothing?"

"No. I can't say I do, not offhand, but I'll think." He paused. "You sound upset. Anything else happen besides Danny landing in jail?"

"That man with the Tidewater Virginia voice stopped when Brace and I were waiting for the light. He started in again about Brace being imprisoned inside his harness. Finally I asked him straight out if he came from Virginia, and he took off with the usual screech of brakes. Pip, I absolutely hate it! I've always felt free to go around anywhere I wanted, and now — now I'm afraid all the time that something will happen to Brace."

64

There was silence from the phone. Then: "Did you tell the police this?"

"No."

"Why not? I don't know much law, but it seems to me harassing somebody who's blind should be some kind of felony or misdemeanor or something."

"I think they think I'm involved with Danny. They think he's mixed up with whatever made Barbara Weldon disappear."

"You know, she could have just taken off one night on a bus to New York. Who could blame her? With a mother like that any kid would."

"Yeah. I guess so. But wouldn't they be looking for her in New York or some other big city? Be watching bus terminals and airports and so on?"

"Probably. Did you tell the police about Meg's cat?"

"No, nor about Jeremy Stoddard's General. I thought they'd decide that Danny had done that, too. Listen, I have to go now and feed Danny's cat. I promised him I would."

"Where's that? I thought that Danny was homeless."

"He is. But he uses that big rock at the western edge of the park as a feeding place for his cat and he says it'll be lurking around there, waiting to be fed. He's afraid that the same creeps who took Boomer and General will take Cat."

"You shouldn't go there by yourself. I'll go with you."

My heart missed a beat, but I said, "I don't want to become dependent on people taking me everywhere."

"I can understand that. But what about Brace? It's him they're after."

"Yes. Okay. Thanks, Pip. That'd be great."

"I'll pick you up in about ten minutes."

Brace and I were waiting on the sidewalk when I heard the sound of Aunt Marion's car. It has a special sort of wheeze when she steps on the brake. I heard the car door slam, then she said, "Whom are you waiting for?"

I hesitated, silently cursing this mixing of worst possible circumstances. She didn't like Pip. And she wouldn't approve of my going to the park to feed the cat, not at this time of day, when it must be dusk. At that moment Pip drove up.

"Hi," he said as he got out. "Hello, Miss Hunter."

"Hello, Pip."

"See you later, Aunt Marion," I said. I picked up my tote bag containing a couple of cans of cat food and a jar of water and went towards Pip's car.

"Jocelyn, I'd like to speak to you before you go."

"I'm sorry. I'll talk to you later. Come on, Pip." And I got in the car and pushed Brace in before she could say anything else.

EIGHT

"What was that all about?" Pip asked, as he turned away from the curb. "I've never heard you talk to your aunt like that."

I didn't answer for a moment. I was shocked by how angry I was. I had deliberately not talked to her about various things, mostly things concerning Brace and Cyrus and animals in general.

"Well?" Pip prodded. And then: "I didn't mean it to sound that way. Don't answer if you don't want to."

"Aunt Marion doesn't particularly like animals. She's allergic to them, anyway. And she doesn't think I ought to go around with you."

"I can understand her not being crazy about our being together, my reputation being what I know it is, especially with some of the old biddies at Saint James. But what's with her and animals?"

"Pip, I don't know. I can't understand it. She's got some kind of thing about them. I think she thinks that the time and money spent on them should be spent on the poor and homeless."

"Mom, in one of her rare lucid moments, said a funny thing about your Aunt Marion once. She said she was a good priest who knew a lot about theology and various other olo-gies. That she was comfortable with systems, but not individuals. And that she had absolutely no self-knowledge whatsoever."

I thought about it and decided it was true. Aunt Marion talked about "the poor," "the homeless," "the rich," and so on. I said to Pip, "That was pretty insightful of your mom."

"Well, Mom studied psychology once, got her doctorate in it, in fact, before she started majoring in alcohol. To change the subject. We're at the park, and the big rock is off to the left. There's no way I can take a car anywhere near it. We're going to have to hoof it."

"That's fine. Since you're with me, I can let Brace off the harness and leash. He can run and play like a dog-dog."

"Do you want me to do it?"

"No. I'll do it. Then I'll put my hand on your arm. That's easiest for me. Okay?"

"Okay."

I bent down and unhooked the harness and leash from Brace. Then I hugged him. "Okay, Bracie, run and act like a dog."

He jumped up and licked my face, then I heard his paws on the ground.

"Madam? My arm is right in front of your right hand."

I picked up my tote with my left hand and put my right hand on his left arm.

"We climb straight ahead and a little up. The ground is fairly smooth, just grass. If they're any potholes I'll tell you."

"Fine."

We walked in silence. I spent the time trying to squash down a feeling of elation and happiness and wondering what Pip was thinking.

"Let's avoid that particular hole," Pip said, leading me slightly to the left.

"How far is the rock now?"

"I'd say about two hundred yards."

"Where's Brace?"

"Running around, inspecting trees, clumps of grass, and generally acting like a puppy.

"I wish I'd brought his ball."

"How would a rubber toy do? I got one on the way to your house. I was going to give it to him when we got back."

"Wonderful! Thanks! I'll throw it for him." I held out my right hand. He put the toy in it.

"Brace!" I called. "Brace!" and I threw the toy.

I heard the sound of the grass swishing, and then Pip said "Good catch! You ought to get him on the ball team!"

We kept on moving towards the rock with me throwing the toy for Brace and taking it from him when he came back to give it to me.

"Well, here's the rock. Now what?"

"We call Cat. Cat! Cat! Come along now. Food!" I took a can from the tote and all the time I was calling I was pulling its top off. "Cat! Here's something to eat." I waved the can around, hoping the smell of the food would carry through the air.

"Come on, let's sit on the shelf," Pip said, and guided me forward. "Here it is." He took my free hand and placed it on the shelf.

I sat down, placing the food beside me.

"Is there any sign of her?" I asked Pip.

"Not yet. What does she look like?"

"I didn't ask Danny, because it wouldn't be any help to me in finding her."

"Right, stupid of me. Well, we'll just wait awhile." Then, "Well, I'll be —"

"Is she coming?"

"Put your hand out."

I put a finger in the food and then held it out. In a few

seconds a rough tongue was licking the end of my finger. "Good Cat, good Cat," I said. I put the can down on the grass and heard the slight sounds of an animal eating. Then I opened the wide-mouthed container of water, and I put that down, too. "What does she look like, Pip?"

"Calico, a little on the bedraggled and thin side, but there's nothing wrong with her appetite."

"I hate to leave her here, with those monsters going around. But she's sort of Danny's, and I don't think I ought to move her."

"Well, my old offer stands, if not with me, then with Jack in the stable. But speak fast, because she's just about polished off the food and is now on the water. Maybe she'll hang around for some affection and conversation. On the other hand, if she's got any brains, she won't."

Slowly, tentatively, I put my hand down and felt the stiff, rough fur. She was bedraggled. I stroked and patted her, murmuring, "Good Cat, good Cat."

"Looks like she might respond," Pip said. And then: "No — experience over impulse, I guess. She's hightailing it back into the bushes and trees. Want me to go after her?"

"No. I have to leave her for Danny. From everything he says, she knows how to hide." I opened up a second can and put it down. "I'm leaving this stuff here, in case she gets hungry again. I don't know whether I can come in the morning or not, but she's got enough here even if I don't."

"I'll come and help you in the morning — oh!"

"What is it?"

"Swimming practice. Well, the hell with it! Who wants to be waterlogged that early, anyway!"

"No — don't. I'll leave this extra stuff here. If I can find somebody to drive me in the morning, I will. But Cat's got enough, even if I have to wait until tomorrow afternoon. And there's no need even then for you to have to drive me here. I can get Meg to bring me."

"If you'd rather have Meg —?"

"You know I don't mean that, Pip."

"Then don't talk that way. Cat's gone. Shall we go back?"

"Fine. Brace!" I called. "Brace!"

There was no sound. "Brace!" I called again. Then, "Pip, do you see him?"

"No. Brace!" he called. "Come on, boy. Stop fooling around."

I stood absolutely still for a moment. Nearly always, no matter how far he ran when he was playing, I could hear something about him, his paws on the ground or happy barks. Sounds. Now there was nothing but silence.

An awful fear shot through me. I jumped off the shelf. "Brace! Brace! Brace!" I was almost screaming.

Pip called again, his voice ringing out. "Brace. Brace."

And then I heard him, his paws coming over the turf. I was so relieved I felt sick. "Brace, Brace, come here, come here." I felt him fling himself at me, jumping up on me, licking my face. I hugged him and realized I was almost crying. "He looks all right, doesn't he, Pip? He's never done this before."

"He looks fine. Stop worrying."

I put the harness on him. "Let's go, Brace," I said. I felt foolish, and realized I must sound crazy. "You must think I'm nuts," I said finally as we left the park.

"After what's happened to you and those threats, I don't think you're crazy. But that's one reason why you shouldn't go to a place like the park alone. Okay?"

"Okay. Thanks."

When Pip dropped Brace and me off we went into the house. I hesitated in the front hall, knowing that Aunt Marion wanted to see me. I didn't want to see her. I was still shaky from those few moments in the park when I thought something might have happened to Brace, and I didn't relish having a conversation with my aunt in which I'd be on the defensive. While I was hesitating I heard her voice.

"Jocelyn, is that you?"

"Yes, Aunt Marion."

"Would you come in here a minute?"

"Come on, Brace," I said in a low voice, and added, "It's a pity you aren't a homeless derelict. Then she'd love me to bring you in."

When I had closed the door she said, "How was Danny? And what did they want him for?"

I took a breath. The question seemed harmless enough. "They wanted him because they seemed to think he might have known something about Barbara Weldon's disappearance."

"Sarah Weldon's daughter?"

"Yes. At least I suppose so. I don't know her mother's first name. You haven't heard about it? It's been in the news."

"I've been too busy to read the paper or listen to the radio. When did she disappear?"

"A few days ago. Her mother was at school making a big racket in the front hall. She said Barbara hadn't been in bed the previous night and she wanted to know if the school knew anything."

"I don't blame her for being concerned. Any mother would be. Did anyone have any idea about what might have happened?"

I hesitated a moment. Lately I'd begun to examine everything I said to Aunt Marion, but there didn't seem to be any booby traps in the question. "No. She's been a lot livelier lately. Meg says she's looked brighter and better, too. Everybody thought — or I guess that's what most people thought — that she'd got a boyfriend. Maybe she stayed out with him, or maybe she just got on a bus and took off for some place like New York. Her mother's such a pain, who could blame her?"

It was obvious that I should have examined that statement more closely.

"That's a terrible thing to say! She and I don't see eye to eye on everything, but she does a lot of volunteer work and I've always admired the way she sticks to her beliefs."

"But she forces Barbara to stick to them, too! She watches her like a hawk. She won't let her meet kids in the hamburger shop because she disapproves of the food served there. And when Barbara goes anyway, she makes her read long tracts from some vegetarian manual."

"I've often thought vegetarianism is the only sensible way. And I'm surprised, with your much-vaunted love for animals, that you don't agree."

Aunt Marion had hit a nerve. I'd often felt guilty about my passion for bacon cheeseburgers when I thought of them as one-time cows and pigs.

"Is that what you wanted to see me about, Aunt Marion?"

"No, I wanted to talk to you about Danny. To see if we could do anything for him. But if he's mixed up at all in Barbara's disappearance, that's something else."

"I didn't say he was. I said that's what they're holding him for." I hesitated. If Aunt Marion could do anything to help Danny then it was up to me to keep the peace with her. "Do you know any good civil rights lawyer who could help him? I thought about Pip's father. But Pip says he's in Hong Kong or Tokyo now."

"I can't tell you how delighted I am to hear you express

an interest in civil rights!" Aunt Marion's voice was suddenly much warmer.

I started to say, I'm not interested in civil rights, I'm interested in Danny — and in Danny's getting back to feed Cat. Instead I smiled. I felt dishonest, but it didn't matter. "*Do* you know any lawyer who might help Danny?" I repeated. And felt bound to add, "For nothing."

"I don't think I do, offhand, but I can look around. I'll let you know."

"Thanks," I said, and meant it. Danny needed all the help he could get.

After dinner, when Brace and I went up to bed, I put him in my bedroom, then opened the guest-room door. The kittens tore into the hall. Luckily I was able to find them and get them back into their room. I cleaned out their pan, checked their water and washed their dishes. After that I played with them a little and finally, before I went to bed, put more food down. I loved the feel in my hands and against my face of their soft, wriggling bodies. Then I checked on Cyrus. In fact, he was checking on me. When I opened the spare bedroom door he was standing right there in the hall grunting softly. I decided to let him in and hope he didn't take exception to the kittens. There was a certain amount of hissing, but nothing more alarming. I didn't want him to eat their food, so I picked him up and put him out, checked to make sure the kittens still had their food, were still eating and in the room, then left them to it. I had saved a small treat for Cyrus, something from a package of goodies that seemed to be irresistible to cats and that Dr. Reynolds approved of. Holding it in my hand, I led Cyrus back into my room, where Brace was waiting for us.

The next morning the school was assembled in the small auditorium while the head, Mr. Borham, known as Old Boring, addressed us. "As I'm sure most of you already know, Barbara Weldon disappeared a week ago. I'm afraid I have to report that nothing has been heard from her or about her since she vanished, which is why I'm talking to you. The police asked me to ask you to try to remember anything that might give them even a hint as to what might have happened to her — anything at all. Even something that would not strike you as in the least important. Also, to keep a watch for anything that might give them a clue. That's really all I wanted to say. Please rack your brains and memories. Barbara's life and . . . and her safety are at stake. And I know you want to help her in any way you can."

"You mean they've heard absolutely nothing?" I asked Meg as we went to class.

"I guess so." Meg sounded miserable.

"Boomer?" I asked.

She shook her head.

Automatically my fingers tightened on Brace's harness, and I felt his response in the way he hesitated for a moment in his step as we went down the hall.

Meg sighed. "Daddy wants me to take a kitten abandoned on a road somewhere that somebody brought in. It's only about four weeks old. It'll be a miracle if it lives. It couldn't even be weaned at this point."

"You sound like you don't want to. Is it because of Boomer?"

"Yes." She burst out, "It sounds crazy, I know, but I have this feeling that if I take my . . . my attention off Boomer, and getting him back, then I really will never see him again." She paused. "Cyrus okay?"

"Yes. I was worried yesterday when he didn't come back and snooze on my bed in the afternoon the way he usually does, but he showed up that night. Do you still think Barbara's probably taken a bus to New York or somewhere just to get away from her mother?"

"I don't know. I guess that's what I'd do if I lived with Mrs. Weldon."

When Jeremy arrived for my lesson that afternoon I told him again, "You didn't tell me about General, but I heard and I'm sorry."

"So am I. Very." He paused. "How are you getting on with the concerto?"

"All right."

"Let me hear you go through the first movement."

As I played, I thought about how things weren't ever the way they were supposed to be. Jeremy was a good pianist and a fine teacher. Artists of all kind were supposed to be highly emotional and given to expressing what they felt. But Jeremy was as buttoned up as British colonels were supposed to be — stiff upper lip and all. Well, if he didn't want to talk about it, he didn't. I concentrated on playing.

When we were finished I got up, and as I did so, accidentally knocked the cassette player containing the tape of the orchestral part of the concerto off the piano.

"Oh," I said. "Did it break?"

"No," Jeremy said. He must have picked it up because he said, "Here, gently does it."

I felt the cassette player, pulling the top up to feel the tape inside.

"Careful," Jeremy said. "It's an old tape."

Hastily I closed the cassette player again. "Did it belong to somebody else?"

"Yes. A former student."

"Anybody I know?"

"I doubt it." He bit off the word. Then added, sounding almost reluctant, "His name was Dominic Renault."

The less communicative Jeremy was, the more I felt like asking questions. "What happened to him?"

"It's really no concern of yours, Jocelyn. I don't know why you ask the questions you do."

"Sorry. I guess it's because talking to you is like talking to a brick wall. If you want to stick to business, business, business, that's fine with me." I felt my watch. "It's now five. The lesson is over. You know your way out. Come on, Brace." I was behaving like a spoiled child and I knew it. The trouble was, Brace wasn't in his harness leading me, so as I stalked out, I promptly fell over a chair. And landed on the floor.

"You left that chair there," I said furiously, rubbing my leg. "I've asked you and asked you not to move furniture without telling me where you've put it."

"I'm sorry, Jocelyn. I forgot. Here, let me help you!"

"I don't need your help, thanks. Don't let me keep you." I knew I was being nasty, but I couldn't help it. Next to my blindness and Brace, music was what I thought most about and felt closest to. Somehow I thought this ought also to include my piano teacher. So when Jeremy closed up, I felt rejected. I struggled to my feet, waiting to hear his steps going out, but he seemed to stay where he was.

"The reason I didn't want to talk about Dominic was that about two years ago he disappeared."

I felt his hands under my arms, helping me up. "Again," he said, "I'm sorry about the chair."

"It's all right."

"About Dominic —"

"You don't have to tell me if you don't want to. I don't know why I've been so snotty. I guess being worried about Brace has something to do with it, and Danny. But I didn't have to take it out on you."

"Why are you worried about Brace?"

I told him about the man with the Tidewater accent and his comments about Brace. "They may not sound like threats, but they've made me feel like he's threatening to do something with him."

"I don't blame you. I wonder if he's the one that took General."

"How did he disappear? I mean, when did you last see him?"

"As you know, I teach in other people's homes. General's always waiting for me — well, he used to be always waiting for me — when I get home. When I got home three days ago the back door was open and General was gone. I know somebody must have stolen him. He wasn't a young dog. He might step out for a minute, but he'd go back in to wait for me."

I heard the sadness in his voice and put out my hand. "I'm sorry, really sorry." I hesitated. "I guess you've talked to all the people — Dr. Reynolds, the police, and so on."

"Of course. And Dr. Reynolds told me about Meg's cat — what's his name — Boomer."

"Did Dr. Reynolds have any ideas about it?"

"Not really, except that I thought he was probably sparing my feelings. The most obvious motive would be to sell him — probably for some disgusting medical experiment."

"Yes, that's what Meg told me he said."

He paused and then said, "About Dominic. He was the most brilliant student I'd ever had. In a way, he was a teacher's dream — practiced hours every day, worked all the time at Rhyder."

"Rhyder?" I asked.

"Yes, the music school in Meridan. I taught there for a while before it ran out of money and closed a couple of years ago."

"I think I've heard of it."

"Well, Dominic was a student there. Spent all his time at the piano. He had an intense nature, made all the more so by an unstable family life. Anyway, his work started falling off. I couldn't believe it at first. I thought he was ill. When I asked him why he hadn't practiced he suddenly yelled at me. Said all I cared about was his music and playing. Not about him. And he slammed out of the room.

"I even went to see his mother — at least I tried to. I found she was on one of her periodic visits to a psychiatric institution. His father was not interested. Anyway, he didn't want to have his son become a musician. Wanted him to go into the family business. Then I talked to Dominic's teacher. She said that she had always felt Dominic didn't have much fun, and that now he was involved with a whole new set of people and she thought it was great! So that was the end of that."

"You never heard from him again?"

"No."

"I'm sorry, Jeremy. Truly."

"It's okay. It took the stuffing out of me for a while and it kind of put a pall on my teaching."

"I don't wonder!"

Jeremy hesitated. Then he went on: "It wasn't just his brilliance and talent. I was — I had become fond of him. Sort of the son I hadn't had. He had all the practical sense of a six-year-old, and I — I suppose I had envisioned us working together. If he got pushed in the right direction, I told myself, there was no place he couldn't go. Well, I got shown, didn't I? Work on that piece, Jocelyn. If you really work at it, you can do a lot with it."

"Am I — could I be as good as Dominic?"

I heard his steps turn from the door. "That's up to you. I told you, Dominic didn't do anything but work. He had a one-direction, tunnel intensity that's rare. I don't know whether you have it — or could have it, or maybe, most relevant of all, want to have it. You're the only one who can really answer that, Jocelyn. You certainly have talent. How far you want to go with it, only you know."

For the next few days Pip came by every afternoon around five and drove me to the park. Cat would always come when we called. Once I took one of Cyrus's brushes and tried to smooth her coat. She wasn't at all crazy about it, and clawed my arm.

"If you're going to turn into the state's leading pianist, you'd better watch your hands," Pip said, taking the brush from me. "I'll try."

"How're you doin'?" I asked a minute later.

"She doesn't like it any better from me than she does from you, but I think she recognizes power when she sees it. There, she looks better. Ouch!"

I giggled. "Some power!" Then, when we were driving back, I said, "Why did you make that comment about me being the state's leading pianist?"

"Because I loitered outside your living-room window a couple of days ago and listened to you. You're good, Joss! You really are. Doesn't your teacher say so?"

"Well . . . he thinks I could be if I applied myself."

"So apply! What's the news of Danny?"

"I don't know. I'm going to go down there tomorrow. He must be worried about Cat and I want to reassure him. Aunt Marion said she'd try and find a lawyer who might help him, but she hasn't said anything."

But the next day turned out to be too late.

When I got in after feeding Cat I checked the tape on which Aunt Marion left me messages when she was leaving the house and found that she was doing an unexpected stint of sleeping over at the church with the homeless in the shelter there. So I decided I might as well go and see Danny that evening.

For a moment I thought I might call Pip and ask if he'd take me, and my heart gave a little jump. I put my hand out to the phone. What if he were busy? Of course he'd be busy — he was known for always being out somewhere with somebody. But he'd postpone his date and agree to pick me up later because I was blind and needed help. . . . Knowing that, I also knew I couldn't bear to take advantage of it!

I felt my watch. Six-thirty. We were still on summer time, so it would be light now. "Come along, Brace," I called, and as I did there flashed through my mind the memory of that hateful voice with the soft accent. I hesitated, then buckled on Brace's harness. I couldn't let myself be stopped by fear.

A screech of tires while Brace and I were waiting for a light to change was enough to send my heart pounding. I found myself gripping the harness. But nothing further happened. I got to the jail and asked to see Danny.

"You're too late, Jocelyn," the detective said. "His uncle came and got him out."

"What uncle?"

"Search me. But he brought identification and a lawyer who threatened to sue if we held Danny any longer. So we let him go. Personally, I still think he knows more than he's saying about the Weldon girl, but we're not going to quarrel with a court order telling us to let him go."

"I didn't know Danny had an uncle," I said. "I mean, he never said anything to me about it."

"Well, I guess he didn't tell you everything."

"Do you have an address where his uncle, or his uncle's lawyer is, where I can call?"

"That's confidential information."

"I bet you'd give it out to another lawyer, or a newspaper reporter," I said.

"Maybe. But you're neither."

Curiously, at that moment, I thought of Pip's question as to whether I'd told the police about the man who threatened me about Brace. Standing there in the police station, I was aware of an impulse to do just that. Maybe one of the cops would offer to drive me home.

"Anything else we can do for you?" the detective's voice said.

"No," I said. "Let's go, Brace."

As I left I heard one of the other officers say, "Do you

have to be so snotty to her? She's only trying to help the guy."

"Yeah. Like her aunt. The poor homeless, victims of society, never mind the fact that they litter the streets, harass people by panhandling and are generally public nuisances."

"Yeah, but —"

"Don't you have anything to do?"

Outside, standing in front of the police station, I felt my watch again. It was now seven-twenty and almost certainly dark. I hesitated, strangely reluctant to go straight home. Was it because Aunt Marion would be out for the night, not returning till after I had left for school the next day? I had never minded being alone before. If I took a detour to the mall, I thought, I could go by the malt shop and have a soda and maybe run into somebody from school. Often Meg and I would stop off there, but since Danny had asked me to feed Cat I hadn't gone. . . . I gave myself a mental shake. I had Cyrus and the kittens to feed. Brace should have his dinner. I had homework and practice. Still I hesitated, reluctant, somehow, to start home. The mall was only a few blocks away, through busy streets. . . . If I went there and had a soda, the whole thing would only be forty or forty-five minutes extra. "Left, Brace," I said, holding out my hand in the signal.

I sipped my malt slowly, one part of me listening for any voices I recognized. A couple of people passing by said, "Hi, Jocelyn."

"Hi," I said in reply, pleased that I could put a name to each voice.

I was in the middle of the malt when I remembered Sandy Martin and wondered if she were behind the counter. Since she was the only person who had ever made me feel her dislike so strongly, I immediately became uncomfortable. And the fact that she'd had a relationship with Pip didn't make me any happier, however much he seemed to regret it at this moment. I finished my malt and slid off the stool.

I left the malt shop and counted my steps until I reached the cassette shop, which I knew was three stores, or thirty steps, farther along. I paused there, thought I might get some new music tapes, but then I decided against it. Time to go home, I thought, and turned Brace in that direction.

I always walk fast, and if I didn't want to, Brace would see to it that I did. He likes to cover ground. But I realized I was almost running as I entered the area where I knew the shops dribble to an end and the houses have not yet started. It's not remote or deserted, and the road is well traveled, but this is not an area where people walk and the sidewalks are pretty empty. Almost without thinking I tracked the cars passing me, their approach and then their streaking off behind me. I was just thinking that it all seemed normal when I became aware of one car whose sound seemed to remain steady and even with my pace. My heart gave a lurch.

Don't be paranoid, I told myself. I could be wrong.

But I wasn't. The unmistakable voice finally came. "Any day now, Brace. You'll be free."

It was no use turning away as I had before. There was no house here. I'd be going into bushes and trees. At least if I stayed on the road there was a chance, however faint, that somebody would stop and help me. I clamped my teeth together and went on. I was being taunted and baited and I knew it. I should have told the police, even that rotten detective. Probably they wouldn't have done anything — at least the detective wouldn't. But one of the others might have. . . . Anyway, there was nothing I could do now except go on. I had made that soft-voiced sadist angry before, and if Pip hadn't come up — I swallowed.

And then I heard the man laugh. "Hurry home, Jocelyn!" He laughed again, the car's engine roared and he shot away, his tires screeching. So he knew my name!

It was a pleasant, cool evening, but I was dripping with perspiration when I got home.

I got out my key and let Brace and me in.

Despite her message I heard myself call, "Aunt Marion?" Of course there was no reply. I stood there in the hall and I knew something was wrong. I was aware of being in a draft. Was the back door open? Jeremy's statement, "The back door was open and General was gone," screamed in my mind.

"Cyrus!" I called. "Cyrus!" I dropped Brace's harness and tore upstairs as fast as I could and into my bedroom, calling for Cyrus. When I got there I ran over to the bed and ran my hand over it. "Cyrus!" I called. "Cyrus!"

Like any cat he could, on occasion, lie perfectly still and listen to me making a fool of myself calling him. But I knew now he wasn't there. It was past dinnertime, and Cyrus should have been sitting beside the paper on which I served him dinner, waiting anxiously to be fed. Or he'd be winding in and out of my legs.

I flew next door to the guest room, my hand out for the doorknob. But there was no doorknob where I expected it to be. The door was open. I went in, walking carefully, hoping, praying to feel the small tumbling furry bodies and hear the squeaks. But I felt nothing and there were no squeaks. The kittens were gone.

I stood there for a moment, stricken and alone. And where was Brace? By now he should have been with me, sniffing around the room.

"Brace," I said. And then, at the top of my voice, "Brace!

Brace!" But there was no answering sound, no bark, no paws on the stairs or behind me.

I ran downstairs, stairs I was thoroughly used to, stairs I had run down before, and tripped on something on the third to last step, and fell flat.

"Brace," I called again, "Brace!" I began to sob. "Please, whoever you are, please, don't hurt him! Please don't take him! Please!"

If Brace had been able to he would have barked at any stranger, which meant — but I couldn't bear to think what it could mean! There was no sound, no reply. After a minute or two I got up and went over the whole lower floor, frantically calling Brace. No response. And I found both the front and back doors were wide open.

I stood there in my total darkness. I opened my mouth and tried to speak. Nothing came out. All I could think about was that Brace had been taken. I was sure the man — the same one who had almost certainly stolen Cyrus and the kittens — had followed me home and somehow silenced and taken Brace while I was upstairs searching for them. Fear, panic, and then grief and rage raced through me. Picking my way, I went to the phone in the hall and lifted the receiver. There was no dial tone. I went back to the kitchen and tried the phone there. It was dead, too.

I don't know how long I stood there, alone, surrounded by silence and my own dark. All I could think about was that Brace was gone. It was what I had feared more than anything, and it had happened. I had known when I got him that in nine or ten years Brace would have to be retired, that he would be too old to continue work as a guide dog. But that was far away and was part of life. This, having him stolen, was like death. The thought that he could be suffering was more than I could bear.

"No!" I said aloud, and started to cry.

But I knew that crying wouldn't get me any further towards finding him. There was no phone. Aunt Marion was at the church. What I had to do was get to a phone, anybody's phone.

I got up, and even though I was in the kitchen, which I knew well, I stubbed my foot against a chair. For a moment I stood, trying to calm myself and to give the pain a few seconds to subside. Careful! I thought. Somewhere upstairs was my cane. It was a while since I had used it, but it was the only mechanism for walking safely I now had.

Sliding my feet, I got to the stairs and started slowly going up. On the third step I found what had tripped me before — Brace's harness. Holding it, feeling it, brought him so near that my sense of loss was like a knife twisting in me. I was scarcely aware of the tears pouring down my cheeks. Finally I got to the top of the stairs and across the hall to my bedroom. My cane would be leaning against the wall just beside the door — unless someone had moved it.

When my fingers closed around it, the relief was overwhelming. Holding it in front of me, tapping the end, I got downstairs again.

Outside the house, I hesitated. I could go towards the neighbors on either side of me. They'd both outdo themselves to help me. The neighbors on the left, I thought, were more likely to be home. They had small children, which tied them down much more than the older family on the right.

Tapping the cane against the ground in front of me, I started across our lawn towards the Pearsons' front lawn, aware that whoever had taken Brace might still be watching me. I had to act quickly. Getting Brace back was the only thing that mattered.

My guess that the Pearsons would be in was wrong. Young children or no, they were all out. With rising anxiety, I rang several times and listened for any sounds coming from the inside — the TV set or voices — in case the bell didn't work. But there was no response. I sent up a prayer that the neighbors on the other side would be in. Turning, I tapped my way back across the Pearsons' lawn, to ours and then across it to the McBrides' on the right and rang their bell. To my vast relief I could hear voices even through the window. There was no doubt that they were in. In a moment the door opened. "Yes?" Then: "Jocelyn? Has anything happened? Come in."

"Brace, my guide dog, has been stolen. Also my cat and the two kittens. My aunt's out, she's at the church for the night. The back door was open and the phone wires have been cut. May I use yours?"

"Of course. My God! How awful. The phone's there," the voice went on, and then hurried ahead of me. "The phone's on the table here, just in front of you."

I called the police first. Unfortunately, I got hold of the detective who had been so unhelpful. "Look, Jocelyn, maybe your dog ran away. Maybe he —"

"He was in his harness. I left him alone because both the front and the back doors were open and I raced upstairs to see if my cat and the kittens had been stolen, and they were, and by the time I thought to call Brace, my dog, he was gone."

"Maybe you left the doors open. People do that. Maybe your cats got out. You know we have a limited number of officers, and we can't send them out for lost animals when people are missing."

"But this is my guide dog!" I couldn't believe the cop was reacting this way. "I'm blind and he's my guide dog. Don't you know how necessary they are?"

"I'm not into guide dogs. Like I said, we're stretched to the limit looking for Barbara Weldon and —"

I hung up and burst into tears.

"What's the matter, wouldn't he do anything?" Mrs. McBride said. "That's outrageous. I'm going to talk to him!"

"He ought to be brought before a hearing for his attitude," Judge McBride agreed. "Let me think whom else we could call."

"Can I use the phone again?" I asked.

"Of course."

This time I called the telephone company and told them what had happened. "Can you send somebody soon?" I asked. "I'm blind and I need to be able to reach people." I hated using my blindness as a plea for special treatment, but this was an emergency.

"We'll send an emergency squad out tonight. Will anyone be there? Are you alone? Would you like us to call anyone? What phone are you using now?"

"I'm using the phone belonging to the people who live next door, Judge and Mrs. McBride."

"All right. Will somebody be at your house?"

"Yes. I'm going back there right now."

"The men should be there in about twenty minutes."

I hung up. "They were a lot nicer than that detective," I said. "May I use your phone once more?"

"Of course. As often as you like."

I hesitated for a moment. Then I called the parish house and asked for Aunt Marion. But I got only a tape recording saying that the church office was closed and would be open tomorrow morning. In an emergency, the rector could be reached at such-and-such a number. I realized that Aunt Marion must already be sitting up with the homeless in the church itself and probably hadn't even heard the phone. So I just hung up.

I dialed Pip's number. A slurred voice answered. I recognized Mrs. Mowbray. "Is Pip there?" I asked.

"I don't think so. He never is. He's probably out painting the town. Who's this?"

"This is Jocelyn Hunter. Could you check and see if he's there? It's very important. Tell him Brace, my guide dog, has been stolen."

"Sure." I heard the phone dropped and steps going away. After a while they came back. "Not here," she said. "What did you say the message was?"

Slowly I repeated, "It's Jocelyn Hunter. My guide dog has been stolen."

"Okay." She hung up.

"Thank you very much," I said to the McBrides. "I'd better get back now because the phone people are coming."

"I'll walk back with you. No," the judge said, as I started to make a sort of protest, "I insist. And I'll sit with you until they get there and you can telephone someone else."

I was glad to have his company, even though, with the best of intentions, he had no idea of how to guide a blind person.

The telephone people arrived shortly after we got home and started working on the telephone. After a few minutes, one of the men said, "Whoever it was cut the wire near the phone, so we'll put another one in. It won't take long. You don't have any idea of who it was?"

"It was whoever stole my guide dog and my cat and kittens," I said.

"Damn! I never heard of that. Who on earth would be such a creep?"

"I don't know. But other people's animals have disappeared too. Meg Reynolds, the daughter of Dr. Reynolds, the vet, had her cat, Boomer, stolen, and Jeremy Stoddard, my piano teacher, had his English bulldog, General, taken."

"I know there's been a lot in the news about the disappearance of that girl, Barbara Weldon. Do you think the two — the disappearance of the animals and the girl — could have any connection?"

"I've been wondering about that, too," the judge said.

"I don't know whether they do," I said, "but I've had some weird experiences lately. A guy's stopped me a couple of times and accused me of exploiting Brace, my guide dog. This afternoon he called from his car and said something like 'Not long now, Brace.' It's awful!"

"He sounds sadistic, or insane, or both," the judge said. "I can't help thinking he must surely have something to do with this. Did you tell this to the police, or that your phone was cut? I don't remember you saying that."

"I'm not sure. I guess not."

"Because although I can't understand the police's attitude, surely they would have to do something — at least send somebody out here to inspect the place — if they knew somebody had broken in and cut your phone wire."

"You see," I said, "when I told the detective both the back and front doors were open and Brace and the cats were missing, he figured I'd been stupid and let them get out and they'd run away."

The telephone man put down the receiver. "Okay, now; the phone's fixed. Are you going to be all right?"

"Yes. I can make some more calls now. Thanks a lot."

After the men left, the judge said, "I still don't like to leave you alone. When do you expect your aunt home?"

I hesitated for a moment, being pretty sure how he would react, then finally said, "She's staying overnight at the shelter. She won't be back until tomorrow morning."

"Then I must insist you come back and spend the night with my wife and me. We certainly can't leave you alone."

"That's very kind of you. But I don't want to leave. I keep thinking I should be here in case . . . in case I hear anything about Brace. Look, let me make a couple more calls. Maybe I can get somebody to stay here with me."

"All right, but I'm not leaving until I am reassured about that. And I still think you should call the police back and tell them about your telephone. I'll be happy to talk to them if you like."

"All right. But let me make those calls first. Please sit down. There's a chair right over there. I'm going to call Meg Reynolds — like I told the telephone man, her father's the vet and she had her cat stolen."

But Meg was out, and her parents must have been out, too, because all I got was their tape. I left a message, telling them what had happened and asking them to call me.

I sat there beside the phone, trying to think whom to call

next, and trying desperately not to think what might be happening to Brace.

In a few minutes the phone rang. It was Dr. Reynolds. "That's a horrible thing," he said. "Have you told the police?"

"They're not interested, Dr. Reynolds. Listen, can you think of anything that could help me to find Brace, any outfit to call?"

"Not at the moment. But I'll certainly rack my brains and let you know. Where's your aunt?"

"At the church."

"What time will she be home?"

"Tomorrow morning. She's staying overnight at the church shelter."

"Shouldn't I try to get her there to stay with you?"

"No, I'll be OK, if Meg could come over and spend the night."

"As soon as she comes in I'll ask her and I'll drive her over. Is anyone there with you now?"

"Judge McBride from next door. He says he's going to stay until somebody gets here to be with me."

"Good. As soon as Meg gets home one of us will call."

"I hate to keep you here," I said to the judge.

"That's all right. I'm glad to do it."

But when the phone rang again, it wasn't Dr. Reynolds or Meg, it was the detective at the police station. "You didn't tell me that your phone wire had been cut," he said.

"No. I forgot."

"That was a pretty important thing to forget, young lady!"

"Not as important as the fact that my guide dog had been stolen, which you weren't interested in!"

"Dogs run away all the time, when people mistreat them, I —"

I hung up and began to cry again.

"What on earth —" Judge McBride got up from his chair and I heard him come towards me.

"That — that creep practically accused me of mistreating Brace, making him run away. Why is he doing this?"

I heard the phone being picked up. "Operator, please give me the police." In a few moments: "Is this the man who has just spoken to Miss Jocelyn Hunter? No, I don't want to hear what you have to say. I want you to listen. This is Judge McBride. I am retired, but I still have many friends in law enforcement. Unless you get out here right away, with an apology to a stricken young blind girl, you are going to hear about your whole attitude in this case. I'll expect to see you here within the next few minutes."

"Thank you," I said, and wondered if the detective would be so mad he wouldn't do anything to help find Brace.

At that point a car drew up in front of the house, a door slammed and feet were running towards the front door. "Jocelyn!"

"Meg!" I said. I stood up. "I'm so glad you're here!"

In a few seconds more feet came into the house. "Heard anything from anybody?" Dr. Reynolds asked.

"Only from the insensitive, moronic detective down at the police station," Judge McBride answered. "I told him I still had important friends in law enforcement and if he didn't get here with an apology and some help he'd hear from them."

"Like Daddy said, he wasn't interested, I guess," Meg replied.

"He called just now and accused me of not telling him that the telephone wire had been cut, and then excused his previous attitude by saying mistreated dogs often ran away."

"He said that?" Dr. Reynolds said. "He's going to hear

from more than just your contacts. By the way," he added, "I'm Dr. Reynolds."

"I'm sorry," I said. "Dr. Reynolds, Judge McBride."

"Retired," the judge said.

"That nerd! That horror!" Meg said.

At that moment I heard another car drive up, there were a couple of slammed doors, and at least two people came into the house.

"Hello, Detective," Dr. Reynolds said. "I hear you really outdid yourself this evening. Don't you men get sensitivity training?"

"You shouldn't have to be sensitive not to say the things he said," Meg commented.

"I'm sorry, Miss Hunter," the detective's voice said. "I didn't fully appreciate what was happening. We get lots of calls about lost pets —"

"Lots of lost guide dogs?" the judge put in.

"As I say, I'm sorry. Now, will you tell me, right from the beginning, everything that happened, leaving nothing out?"

So I told him about the man with the southern accent who first spoke to me in the cassette store about my exploiting Brace, and about the three other times he stopped, including the time when he was getting out of the car and coming towards me when Pip intervened.

"And tonight?" the sergeant said.

"He stopped the car again and said, 'Hurry home, Jocelyn.' And then, when I got home —"

"Okay, slowly now. What was the first thing that struck you as wrong?"

I tried to calm myself and think back. "I guess the first thing was, something felt wrong. Then I realized there was a draft and I thought maybe the back door was open. I remembered then about Boomer — Meg's cat, and General,

Jeremy's — Jeremy Stoddard's dog. I dropped Brace's harness and flew upstairs, went to my room, where I looked for Cyrus, my cat. He wasn't there —"

"Forgive me, but how could you be sure he wasn't there?"

"He's always near his dish when I come home late, waiting for his dinner, and if he's not, he's on the bed. I felt the entire surface of the bed and called and called him. If it's the middle of the day he could be out, but never not having eaten."

"Couldn't he have hunted and found his own dinner?"

"She's presenting her evidence, Detective," the judge said crisply. "Not propounding a scientific statement."

I heard him draw in his breath. "All right, Joce — Miss Hunter." It was marvelous, I thought, how his respect went up when there were men with authority present. "Has he ever not come home in the evening either to get his dinner or when you called him?"

"No. Never."

"And how old is he?"

"Four."

"You mentioned other cats."

"There were two kittens that Danny, the homeless man you were holding, gave me. His own cat had had them and he was afraid that whoever was stealing animals would get them easily. Also, he said there's a raccoon in the park, and the kittens would be killed by it in no time."

"If Danny lived in the park, how could he have a cat?"

"It was a stray, but Danny likes animals and feeds the strays. That's why he wanted to talk to me. So I would feed his cat."

"You didn't tell me that."

"You didn't ask me. You weren't interested in missing animals. You were holding Danny because you thought he had something to do with Barbara Weldon disappearing."

"Were holding him?" Dr. Reynolds said. "Where is he now?"

"His uncle came and got him, with a lawyer."

"Danny doesn't have an uncle. He came out of a series of foster homes. Who was this uncle?"

"I asked the detective that," I said. "But he wouldn't tell me. Danny never mentioned an uncle."

"How do you know he comes from a series of foster homes, Doctor?" the detective asked.

"Because he's occasionally brought one of his strays into the clinic to be looked at."

"And he paid you?"

"Of course not. But since he's terrified of coming into the town I knew what it cost him in sweat and fear to bring it. We did what had to be done."

"And he told you about the foster homes?"

"More or less. I put one or two things he hinted at together and questioned the local child welfare people. They knew him and had known him for years. I'd like to know why somebody wanted him out of jail badly enough to pretend to be a relative. And I'd like to know what on earth made you think he knew something about Barbara Weldon."

"Last time she was seen was near the park. He lives in the park. We thought he might have seen something or known something."

"And you held him in jail for that?" I said. "Poor Danny. He was terrified of being locked up."

"Did you charge him?" the judge asked. "Did you read him his rights?"

"Look, he's a homeless nobody, littering the streets, costing the taxpayer. If he had seen anything, he could have broken the case."

"But you let him go to a man who obviously was not related

to him," Dr. Reynolds said. "What good was Danny to him?"

The judge said dryly, "I suspect because the man who got him out figured the same as the detective did — that Danny might know something about Barbara Weldon's disappearance. And if that's so, the man figured Danny might be a danger."

"But he could kill him and nobody'd know the difference," I said.

"I think that's entirely possible — if it hasn't already happened," the judge said.

After the police and the judge and Dr. Reynolds had gone, Meg and I sat in the kitchen, sipping sodas, not saying much. There didn't seem much else to say.

"What kind of people would take pets?" I said. "I know about selling them for experiments —" I stopped, because the thought was awful. "But are there any other types of reasons for stealing them?"

"Well, there are the nuts — the kind that go around liberating them from zoos and so on." She paused. "Somebody said in class once something about some people making a sort of religion out of it — earth worshipers and so on."

"And they liberate animals?"

"That was the general idea. People have enslaved animals, et cetera, et cetera. . . . Weren't you there when she said it?"

"Yes. Who was it?" I said.

There was another brief silence. Then: "Barbara Weldon," we both said at once.

"My God!" I said. "Do you think she could have anything to do with this?"

There was a pause as we stared at each other.

"Brace and Boomer and Cyrus and the kittens and General have all gone," I said. "And Barbara's gone."

"And the guy who kept threatening you from the car, didn't he talk about animals being used or exploited and so on? Just like Barbara, before she was kidnapped."

"If she was kidnapped. The animals were. But maybe she was part of taking them. Meg," I said, "we have to go talk to her mother. She might know something that would help and doesn't know she knows — if you see what I mean."

"Don't you think the police would have questioned her?" Meg asked.

"But they hadn't put the animals and Barbara's disappearance together. Do you think maybe we should phone her now?"

"Joss, it's after eleven. You know what she's like. Not exactly easy. If we woke her up —"

"But her daughter's missing. Wouldn't that make up for our waking her up?"

"I think we'd do better if we went to see her, brought it up sort of easily."

Reluctantly, I saw the wisdom of what she said. "Okay. I guess you're right. Meg, could you get your father's car? We could cut school and go in the morning."

"Sure," Meg said. And then I heard her give a huge yawn. "I'm sorry, Joss. I'm just as worried as you are. They also have Boomer, and I get sick when I think of what might be happening to him. But if I don't get some sleep I'm going to be out on my feet."

"I'm sorry. Come on upstairs. I'll show you the guest room."

"Can I have a bath first? If I don't take it now, I may not get it in the morning."

"Of course."

It was while she was in the shower that the phone rang. I went into my room and lifted the receiver. "Hello?" I said.

"Hi," Pip's voice said. "Listen, I just heard what happened to Brace and I wanted to tell you I couldn't be sorrier and is there anything I can do?"

"Thanks, Pip. I don't think there's anything. Dr. Reynolds and Judge McBride from next door and even that rotten detective from the police have been here."

"I know you must be tired of talking about it, but can you tell me what happened — just a hasty rundown? The message I got was a little vague."

I told him and added, "Your mother wasn't in the greatest shape when I called."

"She did get the words 'phone call' out, and 'dog stolen,' but I couldn't get any further sense from her. I'm sorry I wasn't here. Sure there isn't anything I can do?"

"Maybe you can help us tomorrow. There isn't a car here. Dr. Reynolds drove Meg here, but we want to go see Barbara Weldon's mother, and we were going to ask Dr. Reynolds to lend us one of his cars for Meg to drive."

"What about school?"

"We're going to cut that."

"Why do you want to see Barbara's mother?"

I told him what both Meg and I had heard her say in class. "Do you remember hearing it?"

"No. That must have been one of the days I cut or didn't make it or something. Wonder what she meant."

"That's what we'd like to find out."

"Okay. I'll come by for you at nine. I was going to . . . but I can break that."

"Don't, if it's something important."

"Nothing's more important than getting Brace back. I'll be there at nine."

"Thanks," I said. "Thanks a lot."

"De nada. See you in the morning."

I was thrilled, but when I went back to the guest room Meg was not. "Well, if he's going to take you, then you won't need me," she said. "I won't have to cut school."

For a moment I was stunned. It was so unlike her. Then I realized why she was acting in such an untypical way. "Meg —" I said. "Think of Boomer!"

"Boomer'll be just as much helped if it's you and Pip as if I were along."

"It's because of Pip, isn't it?"

"Yes. He may be your good buddy, your best pal, but he's a jerk to . . . well, if you're in love with him. He likes to get girls in love with him, and then he likes to leave them flat. If you couldn't go if I didn't drive you, of course I'd go. But —" She stopped. Then she gave another huge yawn.

"Okay, I'll let you get some sleep." I went back into my room, puzzled and a little angry. I felt that the more people who went to see Mrs. Weldon, the more she'd believe us. And with Boomer lost, Meg could be powerfully persuasive. Then I reminded myself that she'd come here to be with me when I needed her and I really had no reason to be angry. I got into bed and lay there, thinking about Brace and Cyrus, longing for them, praying they were all right. I was almost asleep when I heard my door open. "Who's that?" I asked sharply. Then: "Meg?"

"Yes. It's me," Meg said. "Did I wake you up?"

I sat up. "No. What's the matter?"

"I realized what a jerk I was being. I'm sorry. Of course I'll go with you and Pip."

"Thanks, Meg."

But nine o'clock came and went and Pip didn't come.

"What can be keeping him?" I said angrily.

Meg didn't say anything.

Every now and then I felt my watch to check the time.

102

When it was nine-thirty I got up and and was walking to the phone when I heard Aunt Marion's car drive up. "That's Aunt Marion," I said.

"Maybe she'll drive us," Meg said. "I'd have called Dad, but I know he can't leave the clinic now."

I realized I hadn't even thought of asking Aunt Marion to help us.

In a minute or two she came in the front door and stopped. "Jocelyn, Meg, why aren't you in school? Is anything wrong?"

"We're not in school," I said, "because Brace has been stolen, the police have been here, and I think he and Boomer have been taken by that crazy who's been accosting me on the street. And Cyrus and the kittens are stolen. Pip was supposed to be here to drive Meg and me to see Mrs. Weldon because we think that it's all tied up with Barbara's disappearance." As I spoke I was dialing.

"You see, Miss Hunter," Meg said, "that crazy who's been bothering Jocelyn said something like we heard Barbara say in class, something about the animals being exploited and —"

"You say the police have been here? When?"

"Last night," Meg said. "After Judge McBride called and chewed out the detective and Daddy called, too —"

"Stop! Stop! What are you girls talking about? What is all this about police and the judge and animals being exploited and stolen and a crazy person? What in the world's going on?"

Meg and I stopped and looked at each other. Suddenly it occurred to me, and probably to Meg, too, that Aunt Marion really didn't know anything much about Barbara Weldon and the crazy man because I hadn't told her.

I took a deep breath and said, "Well, there was that sadistic nut who kept stopping his car and saying that Brace was being exploited," and I filled her in about the times it had happened in the cassette store and on the road.

"And then we put it together with Barbara Weldon's disappearance," Meg said, "because we'd remembered what she'd said in class once, something about liberating animals."

Between us we finally told Aunt Marion everything that had happened.

"But, Jocelyn, why on earth didn't you tell me all this?" Aunt Marion asked.

I didn't answer because although I was beginning to feel a little guilty about my attitude towards her, I wasn't sure for a moment why I hadn't told her. Then I said, "I didn't think you cared about animals that much. Only the homeless."

"I care about *you*," Aunt Marion said. "I'm surprised — and maybe a little hurt — that you didn't know that. And anything to do with Brace — and I guess the other animals — certainly concerns you. And I can't think why you didn't send someone to get me from the church." There was a short silence. Then she sighed. "But I know I can ride my own enthusiasms and I guess I seem to forget other people's. I'm sorry."

"It's okay," I said. "I'm sorry, too."

At that moment I heard a car stop and a door slam. "Meg, is that Pip?"

"Yes, it is. Let's go."

"But —" Aunt Marion was starting as we left the house. I took my stick but held on to Meg's arm.

"Hi," Pip said. "Sorry about the delay."

"We were really worried," I said. And then: "Are you all right?"

"Fine. Hi, Meg. Good to see you."

"Hi," Meg said.

After we were on the way Meg said, "She was nice at the

end there, but she still really doesn't understand your feeling for Brace, does she? I mean, it's sort of strange."

Pip was weaving in and out of traffic like a racing driver. I couldn't see the traffic, of course, but I could hear the noise and could feel the car switching violently from side to side.

"The other night," Pip said, "I told Mom about the reverend's rather cool attitude towards Joss's Brace, which, considering he was a guide dog, was pretty strange. And she said something that sounded like, 'Well, she had that awful experience when she was a girl.' I tried to get out of her what experience, but at that point she had some more to drink and lost whatever she had been about to say. I tried to bring it up the next morning, but just got a blank stare."

"Did she ever say anything to you about an awful experience involving an animal, Joss?" Meg asked.

"No. . . . I'm sorry, all I can think about is getting Brace back."

After a while the car slowed.

"Is this the street, Meg? I can't see a sign," Pip said.

"Yes. It's hidden by the tree. But it says Wigmore Street. Is that what we're looking for?"

"Yeah, I looked it up before I left . . . before I drove to Joss's."

Left where? I wanted to ask. But it didn't seem important.

We got out of the car, and with Meg and Pip on either side of me, walked up to the front door. Pip rang the bell.

I heard the front door open, then Mrs. Weldon's voice, "Hello. You're Pip, aren't you? And Jocelyn and Meg. Have you heard anything about Barbara?"

"We're not sure," I said quickly. "But we think —"

"Can we come in?" Meg asked.

When we were in the living room Mrs. Weldon said, "What have you heard?"

"Barbara said something in class one day — Meg and I

heard her — about how animals ought to be free. That we — people — exploit them —"

"And you've come about that? At a time when I'm worried sick over what's happened to her?"

I said quickly, "You see, my guide dog's been stolen —"

"Well, that's too bad and I'm sorry, but it's hardly comparable to Barbara's disappearance —"

Meg interrupted. "We think Barbara was quoting a man who has said the same thing to Jocelyn on a couple of occasions, accosting her, and we thought it might just be possible that Barbara knew him, and if she did, we might have an additional piece of information about what happened to her."

There was a silence. "Barbara had made some new friends recently," Mrs. Weldon said finally. "She didn't bring them here, as she ought to have done, but I did see her in the mall on a few occasions, when I assumed she was in school, talking to some young people. I immediately went towards them, but one of them saw me coming and they all just dispersed."

"Did you speak to Barbara about this? Did she say anything?"

"Of course I spoke to her, asked her who they were. She said they had asked her directions. I knew she was . . . well, she wasn't telling the entire truth, but when I taxed her with that she wouldn't say anything more. Then she started going out — without telling me where she was going, or with whom. She just said 'friends' or something like that. She's never done that before. When I tried to reason with her, she said if I bothered her any more about this, she'd leave and never come back. Which she has done," Mrs. Weldon finished in a bleak voice.

"Did she say anything to you about animals?" I asked. "Anything at all?"

"Yes, but I didn't pay much attention."

"Can you try and remember?" Meg said. "It might help a lot."

"How could it help Barbara, or help me find her?"

"If she did run away with these people, and they are the ones who've taken the animals, then maybe we can find her through trying to find them." Something, I don't know what, made me add, "Did she ever get any mail from them?"

"Mail? Yes, as a matter of fact she did."

"Do you remember anything about it? About the envelope? Was there a return address?"

"I don't know. I've always believed a person's mail was private. But I suppose I could go up and look in her room."

"Could I help you?" Meg said. "You know, another pair of eyes?"

"Yes, I guess so. Come along."

Pip and I sat in the living room while they went upstairs.

"Somehow," Pip said, "I don't have much faith in this."

"You don't know," I replied stubbornly, wondering why he had been so late in picking us up.

There was the sound of running feet above and then coming down the stairs. "Joss, Pip," Meg said. "Look at this." She ran into the room.

"What is it?" I asked excitedly.

"Just an envelope," Pip said. Then: "Hold it. It's got some kind of stamp on it, you know, the kind of thing people use with their return address on it. It says, 'Animals Are Sacred.'"

"Is there an address?" I asked.

"No, but there's a postal cancellation mark —" Meg paused. "It's a bit blurred."

"Does it say Meridan?" Pip asked.

"Yes, yes, it does."

"That's the town across the lake," I said, and thought:

where Sandy Martin comes from. And there was something else about it, but I couldn't remember now what it was.

"Well," Mrs. Weldon said, coming into the room. "Do you think the envelope will help?"

"It might," I said.

"What are you going to do?" she asked and then added, "If you think it's any help at all, perhaps we should call the police."

I remembered that detective. "First, we're going to go to Meridan," I replied. And then to the others: "Come on, let's go!"

Meridan is a small town, a village really, about twenty miles from Brinton. "There's something about Meridan, but I can't think what it is," I said. All three of us were sitting in front, with me between Pip and Meg.

"All I know about Meridan is that it's dullsville," Pip said. "The whole place closes up about eight at night. Whatever kids there are come here. I'm not even sure they have a movie house."

"Why's it so different from Brinton?" I asked.

"Well," Meg said, "it's a lot smaller. And I think the townspeople are terribly strict. Church-going fanatics, that kind."

"I wish I could remember that thing I can't remember," I said, exasperated.

"Don't think about it," Pip said. "Maybe if you relax it'll come."

We drove for a while; then Meg said, "The more I see of Mrs. Weldon, the more I sympathize with Barbara, if she did run away."

"She's like Aunt Marion," I commented.

"I'm not sure she is," Pip said, surprising me. "The Weldon woman is just rigid, and not very bright. I think your aunt is bright, but has blind spots. Animals are obviously one of them. Maybe it's because Mom said what she did about your aunt Marion having a horrible experience involving an animal."

"How could anybody have a horrible experience involving an animal?" I asked indignantly.

"Well, they do happen," Meg said. "People who don't know what they're doing buy dogs trained to attack and don't know how to control them. One who was brought to the clinic had killed somebody."

"What was done with him?"

"There was a court order to have him destroyed."

"And did you?"

"We had to. The poor dog was not only trained to attack, he'd been abused. Daddy felt horrible."

"You mean you think Aunt Marion was attacked by a dog and now hates dogs? But when people have been mugged or attacked by homeless people and therefore hate them, she isn't very sympathetic."

"The trouble with you, Joss," Pip said, "is that you have a bad habit of expecting people to be logical. They're not!"

"Thanks a lot," I muttered.

There was silence for a while. Then Meg said, "If the kind of people we think took Brace and the other animals are in Meridan, then they'd stick out like a sore thumb, I should think, Meridan being so proper and old-fashioned."

"How long since you were there?" Pip said.

"About five years."

"Could have changed a lot in that time. You ever been there, Joss?"

"Once," I said. "Driving through. But of course I don't know what it looked like."

"Are you sure you want to go there?" Pip said.

"Yes. If Brace is anywhere there, then there's no question."

"Well," Pip said, after another silence, "we are now approaching the town of Meridan, guys."

"What does it look like?" I asked.

"Like nothing much happens," Meg said.

Pip said, "We're on the main drag — small stores, eateries, cafés and coffee shops, all three of them. An office building. Except for the cars and clothes it looks like it went to sleep fifty years ago and never woke up."

To me it sounded less and less like a place that the man with the southern accent and his friends would be caught dead in.

"Any animals?" I said.

"No," Pip said. "Now that you mention it."

"That's pretty odd," Meg said.

"Yeah. Most small towns have dogs running all over the place."

I felt the car turn. "Where're we going?"

"I thought we'd go back down the main drag and then take the side roads."

"You mean we're through the town? That's all there is to it?"

"Unless it has hidden depths. Hold it —"

"What?" Meg and I said together.

"That guy who accosted you. I only saw his back, but a guy getting into a car in the next block looks like him. Let's see where he's going. Oh, oh!"

"What's happened?" I asked.

"He turned around and saw us. I have a feeling he recognized you, Joss. Can you scrunch down a bit?"

I lowered myself in the seat. "Let's follow him," I said.

"That's what I intend to do . . . damn!"

111

"What's the matter?" I asked.

Meg said, "He turned off the main street, but we've got a red light."

"Let's follow him anyway," I said.

"Your wish, et cetera. Hold on!" And the car was wrenched to the right. "Oh!"

"What now?"

"A cop," Pip said.

"I'm sorry."

I felt the cop's presence by the side of the car. "License?" he asked. Then: "Well, that seems to be in order. Haven't you ever heard that a red light means stop?"

"It's my fault," I said, before anybody could answer. "I'm — we're trying to find my guide dog that's been stolen, and Pip here thought he saw the man who took him. But he turned off and I asked Pip please to follow him."

"Did you know it was a red light?"

"Yes," I said. When backed to the wall, I could never think of a lie fast enough.

"Funny thing. A couple of people here in town have had their pets stolen. That's why everybody is keeping theirs in the houses. What was the make of the car that the guy you thought you knew was driving?"

"A dark blue Ford," Pip said. "And he talks with a southern accent. Sort of Tidewater."

"Don't know anybody around here fits that description," the cop said. "All right. I won't write you a ticket. But obey the light and the other laws, okay?"

Meg said suddenly, "This town used to be larger, about five years ago. I came here once with my dad, and it seemed larger and livelier."

"Well, I guess that was before the music school closed."

"What music school?" I asked.

"Rhyder Conservatory," the policeman said.

"That's what I was trying to remember," I said. "Jeremy — he's my piano teacher — said something about teaching in a music school here."

"It was small, and lost a lot of its students to the bigger city ones, but for a while here it was pretty good."

"Where was it?" Meg asked. "Right in town?"

"No. It was down nearer the lake. Okay, you better go now, the light is about to change again. And remember what I said!"

We drove on. "I guess that blasted Ford is halfway towards Brinton by now," Meg said.

I was thinking about Jeremy and the boy, Dominic Something, the one he taught at Rhyder, hearing in my mind the boy playing the Schumann concerto. It all seemed to be real. "Is the school still there?" I asked.

"Why don't we go and see?" Pip said.

I felt the car turning once or twice and going gently downhill. "Well," Pip said, "there it is. That's got to be what's left of the music school." The car stopped and I felt him put on the brake. "I wonder how we get down there."

"There's a sort of track. I don't think you can see it from where you're sitting, Pip," Meg said.

Pip moved. "Yeah, I can see it. Okay, I'm going down there. You stay here. Meg, you drive, don't you? I'm leaving the keys. If anybody like that maniac comes along, or anybody that makes you or Jocelyn feel threatened, then drive off."

"I'm going, too," I said.

"Listen, Joss. I'm sorry, but that's impossible. I don't want to be responsible for your getting hurt."

"Nobody is responsible for me but me. And I'm going to go. It may sound crazy to you, but if Brace is anywhere down there, he'll know I'm coming, and he'll let me know he knows."

"That's insane," Pip almost shouted.

"Don't yell," I said.

"Have you lost your mind? You can't even walk by yourself. Have you forgotten you're blind?"

"If you don't want to come with me, you don't have to. I do have my stick." And I got it out of my bag where it was folded to about a foot in length and unfolded it. "Meg, let me out." Meg didn't move. I added, "Please!"

"I must be as crazy as Joss is," Meg said, but I could feel her getting out of the car.

"Now, if it's not against your conscience, just point me towards the track," I said.

"Put your hand on my arm," Pip said in a tight, angry voice. "I'll guide you down."

"Thank you," I said. I couldn't squash a feeling of suspicion. "You won't — you won't —"

"Lead you in the opposite direction? It occurred to me, but no. If you're as pigheaded as you seem to be, then on your head be it! Hold my arm! Meg —"

"I'm coming too. You wouldn't recognize Boomer and Jocelyn can't."

"God help us all! All right, here we go."

I held on to Pip but also used my stick to feel the unevenness of the ground. "Where are we going now?" I asked.

"We're walking down the hill towards the buildings. There seem to be three of them, one large and two small, by the lake."

"Can you see anybody?" I asked.

"No," Meg said.

"I don't think so," Pip said, "but I'm not happy about where Mr. Tidewater went."

"Did he go in this direction when he turned away from the main drag?"

"No," Pip said. Then: "Joss, I'm going to say it once more, you shouldn't be here. It's crazy."

"I'm not leaving," I said.

We walked for a while in silence. Then I thought I heard something. "Just a minute," I said. "Everybody stop walking. I think I hear something."

We all stopped. I heard nothing.

"Well?" Pip said.

"No —" And then I heard it again, very faintly, the sound of a piano playing, playing the Schumann that I'd been working on for three hours a day since Jeremy had given it to me. What had been in my head a few minutes before was now happening somewhere outside. "Yes," I whispered. "It's the Schumann."

"The what?" Meg asked.

I could hear it now a little better, as though the wind had shifted. "The Schumann piano concerto. I'm studying it. Jeremy told me that a student of his who had studied it before had disappeared, too."

"What's that got to do with anything?" Pip said impatiently.

"I'm not sure. But when Jeremy tried to find out what had happened to the student, he was told the same thing Mrs. Weldon said about Barbara — that the student, Dominic, had discovered a whole new bunch of friends."

"Maybe — maybe that's Dominic down there," Meg said.

"Come on!" Pip sounded skeptical. "That's really reaching."

"But what if it is?" I asked.

"All right," Pip said. "Let's go on. Of course, anyone could see us coming for miles around."

"Maybe if we moved to the side of the track, nearer the trees?"

"And have Jocelyn stumble over all the roots that are sticking out?"

I knew I was making things much worse — that because of me Pip and Meg could be discovered. But I also suddenly felt a sense of urgency, as though we needed to hurry, although I didn't know why.

"You go on," I said. "I'll wait here. At least you'll have a chance to move more quickly and see if any animals are there."

"And leave you here?" Pip said. "For anybody to walk up to and bop on the head, or kidnap?"

"Take me near one of the trees, the one that has the most leaves left. I'll stand next to it and not make a sound."

"I'll take you back to the car," Pip said.

"No. That'll just take more time." It was hard for me to explain my growing sense of urgency. "Please. I'll be less exposed under a tree than sitting in the car."

"Here," Meg said. "Put your hand on my arm. There's a tree straight ahead that has branches almost down to the ground. That'll hide you."

I followed her over. Pip came just behind me. "If anything at all bothers you," he said, "shout! Shout as loud as you can!"

"All right. Now go."

I don't know how long I sat there. The piano music faded and then grew louder from time to time. Somebody could be playing a record or a tape, of course, but it didn't sound as though it were a recording. Then the piano stopped. I sat as still as I could and kept the image of Brace in my mind. "Brace," I whispered. "Let me know if you're here. Let me know!" I said it over and over again.

Then, almost unbelievably, I heard a bark and I knew it was Brace's bark.

I didn't think. I jumped up and yelled as loud as I could, "Brace, Brace, it's me. Brace!" My stick was still in my hand and I started feeling my way towards the track, not too sure if I could detect it when I came to it.

There were steps behind me, and then more in front of me. The bark sounded a lot closer. "Brace," I screamed. "Brace!"

I turned, warned by a sense of danger. "Goddamn you, you'll pay for this!" a young male voice said close to me. Something leaped past me. There was a yell and the sound of an object, like a body, falling, followed by another sound — that of a car with a siren. In fact, there seemed to be a lot of cars with sirens. I was becoming disoriented and confused, when something hit me on the head and I fell.

I didn't go completely out, but when the roaring stopped and my head cleared, I felt a tongue licking me again and again. "Brace," I said, crying, as I felt him all over. "Oh, Brace!"

"You damn near got killed," Pip said angrily.

"But we got Brace and the other animals," I said. "Where are they?"

"The police and the ASPCA people are rounding them up now, with some of the people down there."

"Would you believe they were having some kind of religious or cult service, and a wretched cat — not Boomer or Cyrus, I'm glad to say — was tied on what looked like an altar?" Meg said.

"Did you find Boomer and Cyrus?" I asked.

"Yes. And the kittens. Your aunt is busy putting them in a box. I just came here to make sure you're all right before I go back and help."

"My aunt? You mean Aunt Marion?"

"She was riding in the police car with the detective and

the other officer. She'd gone to see Mrs. Weldon and found out we were headed for Meridan and they alerted the police. They talked with the cop here, the one who stopped Pip for running a red light. And they got into cars and came here."

"What about Barbara and the other people?"

"It seems Barbara was all gung-ho about the group till she discovered how nutty they were. But when she threatened to leave they wouldn't let her. Locked her in one of the old practice rooms. And she wasn't the only one. She isn't in such bad shape. But some of the others are really freaked out."

"You mean like on drugs?"

"I don't know, but it seems like maybe."

"I wonder if Dominic, Jeremy's student, was among them," I said.

"I don't know," Meg replied. "I guess the police will find out."

I was stroking and patting Brace, whose coat felt matted and dirty. "How's Brace? I mean, how does he look?"

"Filthy. He and the others were kept in a room the size of a closet."

"I thought they were talking about freeing them!"

"Don't try and make sense of it. Some of the animals they did turn loose, poor things. Who knows where they are! The ASPCA man says they're going to put up posters all around the state to see if some of the owners can be located. I'm just glad none of ours were among them. Others they were, quote, freeing for a higher life, close quote, when they sacrificed them in some cult service. They even had leaflets about it. I mean crazy!"

"So that's what that man meant when he talked about freeing Brace for a higher life! He'd have ended up on that horrible altar!" I pulled Brace even closer and stroked him.

"Here's your aunt and the cop," Meg said.

"I'm glad you got Brace back, Jocelyn," Aunt Marion said in her precise way. "And I have your cat and kittens in a box here."

"Thank you," I stumbled out. "I didn't know, I didn't think — I thought you hated animals. And I heard you had some awful experience once."

"I did. I would have denied it until just now — I mean that I hated animals, especially dogs, for that reason. I believed I'd come to grips with it. But . . . I hadn't."

"What happened?"

She sighed a little. "It's not a pleasant memory. On one of my first baby-sitting jobs when I was about fifteen, a dog that had gone mad attacked and almost killed a little boy I was looking after. We had never had any dogs when I grew up, so I had nothing to balance against it. For a long time I couldn't stand the sight or sound of them. I'm sorry for having been so willfully — well, blind, if you'll excuse the expression."

She sounded unsure of herself, which I'd never heard in her before.

"But you don't hate Brace now."

"No. I don't. And he certainly defended you when that wretched man was about to knock you out. He just leaped at him and pinned him to the ground."

I put my arm around Brace. "Good boy," I said, "good boy."

"Well, Miss Jocelyn," the detective, whose voice I recognized instantly, said as he walked up, "it turns out you're quite a detective in your own way. I guess maybe I should have listened to you a bit earlier."

"Did you find Danny?"

"Yes. Not in very good trim, I'm afraid. He'd been locked in a small room. But I did tell him you'd been feeding

119

his cat and he perked up a little. I'm taking him to the hospital."

"Poor Danny." I knew how much he hated going to the hospital. "Is there any chance that he'll come to see it's better to take his medication?"

"I hope so. I suppose I can say that if he doesn't, he can always return to the park."

"I'll go and see him and report on his cat," I said. "What's happening? I hear a lot of people around."

The detective said, "We're getting the animals back to the ASPCA van, and taking the names of the people who are part of the cult."

"Did you get that man, the one with the southern accent?"

"Oh, yes. He won't be bothering animals again for a while."

"Pip," Aunt Marion said. "I owe you an apology."

"It's okay," Pip said.

"But I did see you out last night with a girl."

It was the one bad note in a good moment.

"Miss Hunter," he said, taking a breath, "I was with Sandy Martin because I had reason to believe she knew something about the people here, and I was trying to get some information out of her. Which I did, at the cost of a huge hangover, and that was why I was late. Joss, how do you think I knew about Meridan? She said she thought they had some kind of place here. And she also admitted to having suggested Brace to the guy who seems to run things. I guess the one with the Tidewater accent."

"But why Brace?" Meg exclaimed. "What did Brace ever do to her?"

"Not Brace," Pip said. "Jocelyn. Because . . . because of me."

My heart started beating rapidly.

Pip took a breath. "Because of how I feel about Jocelyn."

"Thanks, Pip," I said, and held out my hand. He took it.

After a minute I said, "And thanks, Meg. Thanks for coming with me."

"Jocelyn," Aunt Marion said, "I have Brace's harness with me. I saw it on the chair when I left and without thinking, I put it in the car. Would you like to put it on him now?"

"I'd love to," I said, and held out my hand for it. Then I knelt down and put it on Brace. It was one of the greatest moments I could remember. I kissed his head. "Come on, let's go, Brace."

And he led me back to the car.